PAPER BUTTER FLIES

PAPER

BUTTER

FLIES

LISA HEATHFIELD

carolrhoda LAB

MINNEAPOLIS

Carolrhoda Lab™
An imprint of Carolrhoda Books
A division of Lerner Publishing Group, Inc.
241 First Avenue North
Minneapolis, MN 55401 USA

For reading levels and more information, look up this title at
www.lernerbooks.com.

Cover and interior images: mimagephotography/Shutterstock.com (face); focal point/ Shutterstock.com (origami); Josh Cornish/Shutterstock.com (trailer).

Main body text set in Janson Text LT Std 10.5/15.
Typeface provided by Linotype AG.

Library of Congress Cataloging-in-Publication Data

Names: Heathfield, Lisa, author.
Title: Paper butterflies / Lisa Heathfield.
Description: Minneapolis : Carolrhoda Lab, [2018] | "First published in Great
    Britain in 2016 by Electric Monkey, an imprint of Egmont UK Limited"—
    Title page verso. | Summary: June is physically and emotionally abused by her
    stepmother, and the only person June feels safe telling is her friend Blister, who
    helps her believe she can escape her nightmare situation, but when a shocking
    tragedy occurs June finds herself trapped, potentially forever.
Identifiers: LCCN 2016053986 (print) | LCCN 2017013043 (ebook) |
    ISBN 9781512482430 (eb pdf) | ISBN 9781512482416 (th : alk. paper)
Subjects: | CYAC: Stepmothers—Fiction. | Child abuse—Fiction. | Friendship—
    Fiction. | Racially mixed people—Fiction.
Classification: LCC PZ7.1.H433 (ebook) | LCC PZ7.1.H433 Pap 2018 (print) |
    DDC [Fic]—dc23

LC record available at https://lccn.loc.gov/2016053986

Manufactured in the United States of America
1-43294-33114-3/9/2017

For Miles—

for making my heart beat that little bit faster.

BEFORE

ten years old

"Drink it." She's holding the glass out to me. It's so full that if she tipped her hand just a bit the water would trickle down the side. "Now."

"But I'm not thirsty." I want my voice to be big, but it's just a whisper.

Kathleen bends so low that her eyes are level with mine. Her eyelashes are black. The blush on her cheeks is too red, like two little apples sitting in puddles of cream.

"Drink it," she says again.

My bladder is full. She hasn't let me use the toilet since I got up this morning and I've already had my glass of warm milk.

I reach out my hand. I wish I didn't touch her cold fingers as she passes it to me.

She watches as I bring the glass to my mouth, as I tilt it against my lips and begin to drink. My throat tries to squeeze shut. My body doesn't want it. But the water flows down and into my stomach.

"All of it." She's smiling at me, the way she does. The way no one else ever sees. As though I'm a mouse caught in her trap and she is the cat and she's got me.

I finish the glass and my bladder is stinging.

"I need the toilet," I say. I know she's heard me, but she's walking toward the sink and turning the faucet on. The glass is filling up. Maybe it's for her. Maybe she's thirsty.

My stomach hurts as she comes toward me. She holds out her cold hand once again and I know what I must do.

I try to drink it quickly, but it's so hard. It makes me ache and it burns my bladder. I step from side to side. She takes the empty glass.

"I really need the toilet," I say.

"Come on, you'll be late for school." Her voice is almost sing-song. "I'll do your hair quickly."

I shake my head. The pain in my stomach is hurting my eyes. Kathleen walks quickly out of the kitchen.

"Megan," she calls up the stairs. "It's time to go."

Then she's back, a red ribbon in her hands. She pulls my hair until my scalp stings. I can't hold my bladder much longer.

"Please, Momma," I say, trying to make my voice so sweet. Trying to sound just like Megan. "I'll be quick. Please let me."

She turns me to look into those eyes.

"I'm not your momma," she says.

Megan is at the bottom of the stairs. She's one year younger than me, but taller already. Her skin is as white as mine is black.

"Quick, you'll miss the bus." Kathleen bends to kiss her. "Have a good day."

I take my coat from its peg and push my arms in. I try not to think of the hot ache in my bladder. If I concentrate on doing up my buttons, picking up my bag, then I can hold it in.

But it's difficult to walk. Every step along the path to the pavement, I think it'll be too late. I look up at the clouds. There's one like an elephant. I trace the shape of its trunk with my finger. It'll help me to forget. I can hear Megan walking beside me, but I won't look at her. I'll look at my elephant.

I'm ten tomorrow, I tell it. It moves slightly and its trunk begins to separate into tiny little pieces.

At the bus stop, there are other children. Megan goes to stand with them. She glances at me quickly.

I move from one foot to the other. I can't hold it in.

The bus is coming. It turns the corner and pulls up alongside us. It's as yellow as the sun. The sun, I tell myself, in the sky, with my elephant. Think of anything, anything but the need to go.

I let them all push each other up the steps. The boy called Greg with the broken nose is laughing so much that I can see his tongue moving. His mouth looks wet, so I look away.

I try to squeeze the muscles between my legs as I walk up the steps. Each movement makes my head pound.

The bus is almost full. I have to take my bag from my shoulder and hold it by my side. There's a seat and I must sit down, but it squashes my stomach and I know I can't hold it.

I scratch my arm, over and over. One two three one two three.

My arm stings, as I feel the wet between my legs. I can't stop it. It soaks my skin and the seat underneath me. I feel it slide its warm path toward my shoes. If I looked down, I know I'd see it on the floor.

I sit still. I don't move even the slightest bit. Just my eyes, which I close and wish that I was anywhere but here. That the seat I'm on would float off through the roof of the bus and take me away forever.

Paula is next to me. She doesn't say a word. Maybe she hasn't noticed. Her face is still pressed tight to the window. The pain in my bladder has gone. But soon I'll have to stand up and everyone will know.

I could pretend that I'm sick. The bus driver would let all the other children off and he'd have to drive me home. He'd ask me why I did it. Why I didn't use the toilet at home, and I'd tell him. Everything. And he'd take me away from Kathleen and I'd never have to see her again. His wife would cry with happiness when she saw me and they'd lead me up to my own pink room, with my own desk, with coloring pencils sitting on the top.

The bus stops.

The children are getting out. The seats are emptying and Paula has picked up her bag and she's ready to move.

"All out," the bus driver calls.

"Move," Paula says.

She knows, as soon as I stand up. I look back at the seat and the material is soaked through.

"Ugh," she says, loud enough for others to turn and look. I put my bag on my shoulder and walk down the aisle. The wet sticks my skirt to my legs. I know that there'll be a big dark patch. The smell is sharp and sits on my tongue.

I want to hold my head up, but I can't.

"Ugh. Stinks of piss," Ryan says. "Was it you, Lauren?"

"No!" she laughs, and swings her bag toward his head.

"Well, someone's pissed themselves." He ducks again, just in time. And he must see, because there's a prod on my shoulder and although I don't turn around I know it's him.

"Oi, Juniper. You've wet yourself."

"My name's not Juniper," I say quietly as I keep walking.

"You stink." And the girls with him laugh.

My wet legs rub against each other as I walk. With every step, my ankles can feel the stickiness. The canvas of my shoes rubs against my skin.

"Do you need a diaper?" Ryan says. I won't look at him. I can't let him see that I want to run far away from here.

We go through the school doorway and the corridor is swirling with people. I think I might cry, but I won't let myself.

"Ugh!" the girls from the bus shout loudly. They squeeze their noses with their fingers. "Someone's wet themselves." And they're pointing at me and everyone is laughing as the bell rings.

"You'll have to come to class now," Ryan says. "You don't want to get into trouble, do you?"

Somehow, I get to the classroom. Miss Hawthorne is already here. She's sitting on her chair, talking to the children on the carpet in front of her. I go to my peg, take off my coat and hang it up. I hang up my bag too. When I turn around, all I can see is them pointing and sniggering and waving their fingers under their noses, their voices screwed up in disgust.

"What is it?" Miss Hawthorne asks. Her smile is warm, but she looks confused. My feet won't move. I don't know what to do, where to go.

"June had an *accident*," Cherry says. They're all laughing and looking at me. The smell of what I've done stings my skin.

Miss Hawthorne comes toward me. She knows, as soon as she comes close, that it's true.

"Come with me, June." We step outside the classroom, all eyes watching. Miss Hawthorne closes the door so they can't hear us. And so I can't hear them laughing. I look down at the floor. I feel myself blushing violently, but she will barely see it through my skin. I wish I could sink into the ground and never come back.

"What happened?" she asks kindly.

"I couldn't hold it in."

"You should have gone before you left home."

"Sorry." I won't cry.

"You'll have to go to the nurse. She'll sort you out with clean clothes. Then you can come back to class," she says. I look up at her. "I know it'll be hard, but you have to come back. They'll all have forgotten about it, you'll see." Her hand is on my shoulder and she's smiling, but I know she's lying.

It's quiet in the corridor. It's just the sound of my feet, soft on the floor. I could walk along here, turn the corner, push open the door and never come back. I would survive—I know I would. I would hitchhike all the way to the coast and I'd meet a family on the beach. They would love me and they would be mine.

The nurse's door is slightly open and I barely knock before I go in. The nurse is standing by the chair, shaking a thermometer. A girl sits with a bowl on her lap. Her skin is so white she looks dead, and I know I shouldn't stare.

"I'll get the office to phone your mother," the nurse says briskly. "She'll have to come and pick you up."

"She's at work," the girl says.

"Well, she'll have to come back."

The girl nods and hunches further over the bowl. The nurse squeezes past me, heads out of the door and is gone.

"Are you OK?" I ask the girl. She looks up at me briefly and turns away.

The window is pushed halfway up. Somewhere, someone is mowing a lawn. The hum stretches into the room.

I can hear the nurse coming back before I see her. Her shoes click on the polished floor.

"Right. That's sorted," she says. And then she turns to me.

I could tell her, tell her the truth, tell her everything.

"I need some clean clothes," I whisper. And now I know that she can smell my damp ones.

"Right," is all she mutters as she reaches into a cupboard. She holds up some underpants and chooses a pair. "A little bit small, but they'll have to do." She passes them to me. "Come over here and I'll draw the curtain."

I do as she says. I pull my wet underpants down. I don't know what to do with them and she looks like she doesn't want to touch them, so I put them on the floor.

I step out of my skirt. The material is damp to touch. I don't want to look at the size of the wet patch that everyone has been laughing at. My shoes feel sticky. And the smell is glued to my skin.

"Let's wipe you down a bit," the nurse says. She's at the sink, squeezing out a cloth and then using its warmth to clean me.

When she's dried me, she helps me into another skirt. It's tight over my legs and on my belly. I know what she thinks. It's what everyone thinks.

The nurse picks up my clothes and puts them into a plastic bag. She ties a knot in the end of it and passes it to me. I'll have to walk through the corridors holding it, but I can't throw it away. I can't go home without it.

"Thank you," I say, and I look hard into her eyes. *Please ask me*, I beg her. *Ask me now and I'll tell you everything.*

"You're really a bit old for this," she says. "Try not to let it happen again."

And I'm gone, walking back to the class of circling sharks, my bag of clothes waiting to be hung like bait on my peg.

. . .

I wake up early the next morning, because it's my special day. I imagine plucking the butterflies out of my belly and putting them in a box by my bed—I'd like to watch their colors, to see their wings beating against the glass.

The door opens and they're all here. Kathleen, Megan and Dad. He promised he'd go into work late this morning.

"Here's the birthday girl," Kathleen says. Her hug is tight and smells of soap. She kisses me on the top of my head.

"Ten years old today!" my dad says. "Here, hold this." His smile takes over his whole face as he passes me the end of some string.

"That's all you're getting!" Kathleen laughs, and my dad puts his hand in hers.

"Follow it," he says. So I get out of bed and I pull on the string and I twist it into my palm as it leads me from my room.

It goes into Megan's room and over her bed. They watch me from the doorway as I step over the mattress, pulling my nightdress over my knees. They all laugh excitedly as I follow the string around the chair and back out again.

"So it's not in there," my dad laughs. I don't look at Kathleen and Megan. I don't want them to spoil this.

The string goes down the stairs, into the kitchen. I gather it clumsily in my fist as I crawl under the table. Back across the hallway, into the living room.

And there it is.

Attached on the end is a shining new bike. It's painted pink, with yellow handlebars. For a moment, I think my heart stops. I look up at my dad and try to speak. He puts his arm around my shoulders.

"It's all yours, pumpkin. You deserve it."

"You sure do," Kathleen says as she takes my hand and we go toward it. "Do you like it?"

"Yes." I nod my head, over and over. "Can I touch it?"

My dad laughs. "Of course you can—it's yours."

It's mine. It's really mine.

I trace my fingers over the handlebars, down its cold frame and across the seat.

"It's got a bell," Megan says excitedly.

"Yes," I say.

"Well, you haven't got time to try it now," my dad says. "But I promise I'll take you out on it tomorrow." He leans over to kiss Kathleen. "I've got to go."

I follow him to the front door and try to hold on to his hand as he puts on his coat.

"Save me some cake from your birthday tea," he smiles. He picks me up and holds me, my feet hanging not far from the ground. "Your mom'd be so proud of you," he whispers into my hair.

Then he puts me down, quickly picks up his bag and is out the door before he can hear my reply.

"Thank you for my bike," I say quietly, and I imagine him smiling back.

. . .

"Was it you?" the bus driver asks when I step on. I look around and pretend that he's not talking to me. "You decided to use my bus as a toilet?"

I shake my head.

You were going to save me. You were going to drive me away and I'd live with you and your wife.

"It was you." Lauren pokes me as I keep on walking. "You've got underpants as stinky and wet as a fish." All around me, people pop their mouths open and closed like a million stranded fishes.

When I sit down, the boy next to me gets up, pushes past me and is gone.

I try to think of my new bike, sitting waiting for me at home. In my mind, it glows. And my dad is going to take me out on it tomorrow, just me and him.

"No one likes you," the voice hisses from the gap in the seats behind me. I recognize it straight away. It's Megan. I hear Anne giggle next to her.

I move along, so that I'm sitting next to the window. Outside, I look at the fields, blurring by in a patchwork. I'll get on my bike and ride so far until I get so lost that I can't find my way home.

"Everyone hates you."

But I won't be scared. I'll be happy. And then my dad, who's been looking for me, will drive past me and stop.

I've changed my mind, he'll say. *Three years is enough time to live with Kathleen and Megan and now I want it to be just you and me. I've bought a new house. It'll be just us.* He'll put my new bike in the back and we'll drive and drive until no one else can find us.

"You'd be better off dead," Megan says.

• • •

We all sit cross-legged on the carpet.

"So," Miss Hawthorne says, "we have a birthday today."

I feel the blood rushing up my cheeks as she smiles at me. I wish she didn't know. She thinks that she's being nice, but I don't want to do this.

"Come up to the front, June." She pats the empty chair beside her.

She doesn't hear the air-popping noises that have started again. I stand up awkwardly, step over the knees of those sitting in front of me.

"Now, remember, don't sit down on it," Miss Hawthorne says. "This is the one day that you're allowed to stand on a school chair. Make the most of it."

I step onto the wooden seat. I'm worried that the people in the front can see up my skirt, so I smooth it down with my hands and keep them clasped there.

"Fishy," I hear someone hiss.

"Right. On three," Miss Hawthorne says. "One, two, three." And they're singing, all their faces tipped up toward me. Ryan moves his hand, as though it's swimming through water, so subtly that Miss Hawthorne would never know. Stuart looks like he's singing, but he's not. His wet lips are just smacking open and closed in a circle, like a dying fish. But all Miss Hawthorne can hear is the sound of their voices, making my day special.

I don't want them looking at me. I don't want any of them looking at me.

As soon as they finish, I get down from the chair and hurry back to my place on the carpet, willing a tornado to suddenly break through the sky and whisk us all away.

● ● ●

"What did you get for your birthday?" Jennifer asks. We're sitting on a wall, safely away in the corner of the playground. Our legs swing down, sandwiches balanced on our laps.

"A bike," I tell her. I'm so proud. I just want to get home so I can see it. Even if Kathleen will be waiting.

"Lucky you." Her red eyes widen, as she pushes a strand of her snow-white hair from her lips. "What's it like?"

"It's pink." I take a bite from my sandwich. The tuna paste is sticky on the bread. "It's beautiful," I say, my mouth full.

"I only got a watch when I was ten."

"That's nice too," I tell her, but she just shrugs.

There are two of them, working their way over toward us. Two girls from the year below, their hair in identical bunches on their heads. They look behind them briefly, but keep walking.

Jennifer stares at them as they stand in front of us. I've never spoken to them before and I don't know what they want. I pick at a piece of bread that's stuck at the top of my mouth.

"We've got you a birthday present," the blonde one says. She's smiling, as though she means it. But this feels wrong.

The smaller one thrusts a paper napkin toward me. There's something wrapped inside.

"Thank you," I say, although my breath feels heavy. I don't want to look up to see who's watching. I'm going to just play along with their game, so they can't beat me.

I hold my head high as I peel back the napkin. One of the girls screams and they both run away.

The goldfish is lying dead. The perfect circle of its eye stares up toward the sky. Its tiny mouth is open in a desperate pout.

They killed it, just for me.

"Fishy!" The shout stumbles across the playground. I knew Ryan had been behind it. I won't look up. Instead, I wrap the dead fish back up and put it gently in my bag.

• • •

Miss Hawthorne is standing by the door and she stops me when I go in.

"June, I need a quick word." I wait outside the classroom as she settles everyone down. The walls of the corridor are very white, as if I'm in a tube of light.

"Right," she says, clicking the door shut. "I need to look in your bag."

"Why?" I ask.

"Some of the children have told me that you've done something you shouldn't have."

My stomach feels heavy. I had only kept the fish because I'd wanted to bury it. It hadn't felt right to throw it in the garbage can. Not when it died for me.

Miss Hawthorne doesn't have to look for long. She picks out the paper napkin with the soft fish inside.

"Why?" she asks me. Her voice is gentle. She's not angry.

"It wasn't me," I tell her. But she just shakes her head.

"A lot of the children saw you do it. They're very upset."

"It wasn't me," I whisper.

"Lying will only make it worse." There's such disappointment in her voice that it almost makes me cry.

"I'm not lying," I say, but I can tell by her eyes that she doesn't believe me.

"I've got no choice. I've got to take you to Mr. Cleadon."

I nod at her. It's easier this way.

I feel so alone, even though Miss Hawthorne walks beside me. I thought I could trust her. I thought one day I'd even tell her about Kathleen and she'd save me. But now I know she never will.

I look outside the windows as we walk. The clouds look like a pixie, but it's hard to see, because soon we're gone.

• • •

"Close your eyes," Kathleen says. Megan and I have barely walked through the door when she's fussing around us, taking our bags and coats and hanging them up.

She stands behind me and covers my eyes with her hands.

"Walk forward," she says, so I shuffle in the direction of the kitchen. "Ta-da!" She takes her hands away.

The table is covered in birthday food. There's jelly and sandwiches and cookies. And, in the middle, an enormous, round chocolate cake, dotted with candies.

Megan seems confused as she looks at Kathleen.

"It's her birthday, sweetie," she says. "Have a look at the cake. I made it myself," she smiles.

I step toward it. There's a new tablecloth, and balloons tied to the chairs.

"What do you say?" Kathleen says.

"Thank you," I reply.

"Come on, let's light these and take a photo."

She holds a match to all ten candles. It's my cake and it's beautiful.

"Blow them out and look at me and smile."

I puff out my cheeks and my smile is real as I look at the candles and blow out the flames into little streaks of smoke.

"Let's eat, then."

We all sit down.

"There's soda too." She smiles, pointing to my cup.

"Thank you," I say.

"Let's start with the cake." She cuts a big slice and tips it onto the plate, then passes it to me. "Don't wait for us."

I hesitate with my fork, but it's too tempting. Chocolate cream oozes out between the sponge. The taste makes the world feel better.

"It's a good one," Kathleen laughs as she eats a mouthful. And it is. Mouthful after mouthful is delicious, until my plate is empty.

Kathleen puts another slice on my plate. I look up at her and she nods at me. Maybe this is the day she changes. Maybe she'll put her arms around me and say she really does love me and she's sorry. I smile back. A little bit of the grit in my heart feels like it's floating away.

I eat my cake, the chocolate filling my mouth. Megan stares at me, but I don't care. Kathleen can love me too.

I run my fingers along the crumbs on my plate, smudging dropped bits of chocolate cream.

"More?" Kathleen asks.

I laugh slightly. "I need to leave space for a sandwich."

"But the cake isn't finished." Just like that, the look is back. Her eyes burn into me.

She puts another slice on my plate. I look down at it. If I eat it, I'll feel too sick to remember the special taste.

"Eat it," she says. Megan looks at me. She has a glimmer of panic in her eyes.

I pick up the fork and push it into the cake. Slowly, I spoon every last bit into my mouth, until I'm sure I'll be sick.

"Have a drink," Kathleen says. I want liquid, but it's too sweet.

"Eat." There's more chocolate cake on the plate in front of me.

"I can't," I whisper.

"Eat," she says.

"I'll be sick."

She's beside me so quick that I jump back.

"If you vomit, you'll eat that too."

I pick up the fork and force the cake into my mouth. I gag slightly and I have to work hard to make it go down. My stomach is cramping—it doesn't want it.

"She's disgusting, isn't she?" Kathleen says to Megan.

"Yes," Megan agrees.

I don't want to cry, but I can't stop myself. I can feel the tears rolling uselessly down my cheeks.

I want to see my bike. I want my dad to come home and take me away from here.

The sweet smell sweeps through my nose. I gag again and am almost sick. The salt from my crying is in my mouth too.

"More," I hear her say. My fork scrapes the plate and goes past my lips, again and again and again, until I have to stand up and run for the bathroom.

I won't be sick, I can't be sick. I lock the door before she can get to me and I curl up on the floor. Everything hurts. My head feels like it will crack open. My stomach is filled with a thousand burning bricks. My throat is sandpapered raw.

I lie on the floor and I cry and I cry.

I want my mom. I want her to come out of the water and come back to us. And my dad will love me enough and Kathleen would never exist.

There's a tap at the door, so gentle.

"June?" It's Kathleen's voice trickling underneath it. "Happy birthday."

• • •

My dad is keeping his promise. He has to get his bike from the back of the garage, but I don't mind waiting. I'd wait all day if it means I can get on my bike.

Kathleen stands in the front doorway. She's leaning on the frame, her arms crossed in front of her, a big smile on her face.

"Do you need help, Brad?" she calls out. He doesn't reply. There's clattering coming from the garage and I doubt he can hear her. She shrugs. "I guess not." She smiles at me.

But there's something, just at the back of her eyes, that I can see. I look away. Out here, I'm safe. Just by being here, my dad protects me.

He appears from the garage. "Sorry, pumpkin. Took me ages to find the pump."

"That's fine," I say. His front wheel looks a bit crooked.

"Are you sure you're all right on that?" Kathleen asks.

"It's straight out of the showroom, this beauty," my dad says, slapping the frayed seat and laughing loud enough for the birds to hear. "Ready, June?"

"Yup." I begin to put my foot on the pedal, when I see her out of the corner of my eye, coming closer.

"No going too fast," Kathleen says. She hugs me and kisses the top of my head. "Look after each other."

"We will," my dad calls as he wobbles off down the road. I go after him quickly and I don't look back.

My bicycle makes me free. The wind pushes against my cheeks and arms. My legs pedal around and around and around and I'm so happy I could fly.

"You're all mine," I whisper to my bike. The whir of its wheels calls back to me. It loves me too.

The road disappears beneath my feet, taking me further away from her. I want to call to the clouds, shout out to the sky.

I watch my dad not far ahead. He's hunched over, looking forward. He's my dad and he gave me this bike and I love him love him love him.

His T-shirt moves slightly in the wind.

Today, I'll tell him. Today, I'll tell him everything.

He turns off to the left, toward the path by the river. My heart squeezes cold and I want to stop.

"Not this way," I say, but I'm not loud enough for him to hear.

It's bumpy under our wheels. I can see the river in the distance, a thick line of black. I never admit to him how much I don't like coming here.

He looks back briefly and tries to put his thumb up, but it makes him wobble, so he carries on looking straight ahead.

The water is here and my dad follows the path, so that the river runs along the side of us. I won't look at it. I won't hear it. I'll see only his wheels going around and around. If I go slightly to the side, I can see the spokes spinning so fast that they almost disappear.

I know we're not far.

I see it in the distance and suddenly I can't and won't take my eyes away.

I love you, Mom.

I hadn't meant to cry today. It's difficult to see, but I can't wipe my eyes without the bike toppling.

The little wooden statue of a heron, stuck tight into the grass, looks out, motionless, over the water. I can see the flowers that Dad and I tucked next to it.

My fingers pull the brakes and my bike slows until I'm right next to my mom's heron.

Up ahead, I hear my dad stop. The path crunches louder as he makes his way back. I look up at him.

"Our flowers are dying," I tell him. The petals are curling, their colors fading.

"They've been here a week," he says.

"I wanted them to last longer." They were for my mom, three different bunches, for each of the years without her.

My dad leans over to try to hug me, but our bikes make it awkward and his arms are heavy.

I won't look at the water.

"Shall we keep going?" my dad asks. He's sad and this was our happy day. I nod, even though I want to stay here, with my mom's heron staring out, looking for her.

He begins to pedal slowly away and I stay close behind him.

"Shall we go to the High Point?" he calls over his shoulder.

"Yes," I shout back.

It's not far to bike and the bottom of the hill is close to the path.

"There's no way I'm biking up that," my dad laughs. It stretches green and steep, the war monument perched proudly on the top. "But I'll race you!" And he's off, way ahead of me.

"That's cheating." I put my bike down gently next to his and I'm running like a leopard. I'm getting closer to him. My legs ache and my breathing burns, but I love it. I push myself faster, but he gets there first. He's lying on his back, his stomach going up and down so quickly.

I fall down next to him.

"You need to get fit," he laughs. "Less eating so much party food and more exercise."

I hold my breath.

The thought of chocolate cake creeps up my throat.

"I'm glad your friends came over though," my dad says. He stretches out on his side and leans his head on the triangle of his arm. "So it's getting easier, is it?"

I look down at the grass. I pick a blade and another. Picking them and just throwing them away.

"It's not going to change overnight, honey, but having a few friends over for your birthday is a start."

Tell him. There were no friends. It's all a lie. But my head can't seem to start the words.

"Kath tried so hard to make it good for you." He sweeps his palm gently across the top of the grass. "We're lucky to have her, aren't we?" When he looks at me, I know I can't say it. He's got a happiness in his eyes that was burnt out when Mom died. "I don't know what I'd do without her."

"I wish I had skin your color," I say. I don't know why that suddenly comes out now. And it's sort of not true. Not all the time, anyway. I got my skin from my mom and I want to keep it.

"Oh, honey." He puts his arm out for me and I curl into him and suddenly I feel so safe. I want to stay lying like this forever, where no one can touch me, no one can hurt me. "Have other kids been saying things again?" I don't move. I don't nod, or shake my head. Nothing. "I know it's hard, but you've just got to ignore them. You're a beautiful little girl.

Every part of you—your brown skin, your big smile, your eyes like perfect chocolate buttons that I want to eat every time I look at you."

He pretends to eat my cheek, but it tickles and I squirm away.

"I wish I had long, blonde hair," I say. "And it'd be so straight."

"No, you don't want that," my dad says.

But that's what she's got, I want to say. *You love Kathleen because of her hair.*

"You see, hair like yours is special. You don't want to be one of the crowd. It's good to stand out. To be a bit unique."

No. I want to sit on the bus with blonde hair. I don't want Ryan sticking pencils in it, because he says they'll get stuck. I want to walk down the corridor without them making bird noises at the bird's nest of my hair.

"You are so like your mom," my dad says. "She learned to keep her head held high and that's what you're doing too. You're worth something, June."

I press my head into his chest until I find his heart, the steady beat of it. Yes no yes no.

I can't imagine that my mom's heart stopped. If it had just kept beating, she'd be here with us now.

I move onto my back and stretch my arm out. If I concentrate really hard, I can feel her fingers in mine. There they are. The warmth of her palm. She strokes my thumb with her own.

Oh, Mom, I miss you.

"Come on." My dad jumps up suddenly. He tugs at my arm and I stand and we walk hand in hand to the monument at the very top. We step onto the stone base and turn to look down over the land. We're giants and this is our kingdom.

The sun is so warm on my face, my arms, my bare legs. Below, there are tiny fields and houses that I could balance on my fingernails.

Somewhere, Kathleen is the size of an ant. I lift my foot and stretch it out. I see her raise her hands and I smile as I bring the sole of my shoe down hard on her face.

My dad laughs. "What are you doing?"

I close my eyes as he puts his strong arm around me. It's just me and him now. Together we can conquer the world.

BEFORE
four days later

"It'll only be for one night."

"But I don't want you to go." Fear grips me. Dad's never gone and left me in the house with Kathleen and Megan overnight.

"I have to. I have no choice." He's tucking me into bed and stroking back my hair. He'll be gone by the time I wake up in the morning and he won't be back until Friday.

"Can't I come with you?" I ask. "I'll be really quiet. They won't know I'm there."

"You've got school to go to."

"I could miss it. It's just two days. And I'll work really hard to catch up."

"Pumpkin, you can't. There's no way around this. But it's not for long. And you'll have a lovely time. Kath has got lots of nice things planned."

I go cold all over and turn toward the wall. My head starts to pound and I know I'm going to cry.

"Come on, June, don't be like this. Some dads have to go away quite a lot. This is the first time I've had to do it."

But I pull the covers high over my head.

I feel the mattress lighten and I know he's gotten up. There's a pressure on my back where he must have put his hand. Then it lifts and I can hear him walking gently across my bedroom floor. The door opens and it clicks closed.

He's gone.

And I didn't let him kiss me goodbye.

. . .

I know that it's Ryan pulling my hair. On and on, while Miss Hawthorne sits talking to us. She doesn't notice. She's too intent on telling us about the angles of a triangle.

"Oi, Juniper." He's shuffled forward and is whispering in my ear. "Caught any fish today?"

I keep staring toward the front. I watch Miss Hawthorne's mouth move, but I don't hear many of her words.

Kathleen didn't do anything bad this morning. She woke me up and I got dressed. My heart had been knocking against my skin.

As usual, she'd put the big mound of food out for my breakfast. Muffins and bacon and thick white bread with chocolate spread. Megan had stared at me, as she always does, as she ate her normal bowl of cereal. Sometimes, she looks like she hates me, but at other times she seems frightened to even breathe. I looked away from her and kept my eyes down for the whole meal. Waiting.

But nothing.

Kathleen had tied my red ribbon in my hair and she gave

Megan her kiss goodbye. She'd told her she loved her, that she was the most special girl in the whole world, and then she'd shut the door behind us.

Maybe, maybe it'll be OK.

We'll eat our meal tonight and watch TV.

"Your breath stinks of sewage," Ryan tells me.

Miss Hawthorne jumps up. "So, if you get into pairs, we can start," she says.

There's a rush of movement, a frenzy of worry from the other children. Jennifer and I go to a table and sit together.

"Haven't found anyone, Ryan?" Miss Hawthorne asks. "You can work with me." Jennifer pinches my arm and I smile at her. Pink pushes itself onto Ryan's cheeks and happiness spreads slowly through my bones. He sees how much I'm smiling, but I don't care.

Miss Hawthorne hands out the paper, so in our pairs we can begin.

• • •

I'm walking to the lunch hall when I'm grabbed from behind. A hand goes over my mouth and I'm dragged around the corner, my feet kicking on the ground. Other children see, but no one helps me, no one stops them.

The main restroom door bangs open and shut. Ryan and Cherry pull me to the ground and Lauren puts a hand over my mouth.

"If you scream, your life won't be worth living," Lauren says. Ryan is getting something from his bag. It's a small pot, and when he cracks the lid off it I can smell that it's paint. Cherry passes him a brush and he dips it in. I thrash my head from side to side, but I can't get away.

The white paint is wet and cold on my cheeks. Ryan brushes it over my forehead, across my chin and over my mouth. The chalky taste drips onto my tongue.

They hold my legs down as they brush the skin on my arms, painting me white.

When the pot is empty, Ryan drops it into the trash can.

"You look like your albino friend now."

He turns his back on me and I hear the faucet turn on and the water splashing into the sink as he cleans his hands. Lauren and Cherry get up and clean their hands too, while I lie motionless on the floor.

Ryan looks back at me before he goes.

"A big improvement," he says.

They're gone.

It's totally quiet.

I look up at the ceiling, at the squares of foam bricks held together with strips of metal. I could lie here forever.

A noise outside makes me scramble to my feet. Two younger girls come in and they scream when they see me and run out giggling.

I won't look in the mirror. I won't see what they've done to me. I won't see myself as their dream of white. I'm my mom's color and I always will be and that's what I want to be.

I turn on the faucet that Ryan touched and let the water wash over my arms. My skin comes back. I scrub at my face and work the paint from strands of my hair. I rub some wet tissues over my legs, until every last speck of the stinking white has gone.

And, just like my mom, I hold my head high, push open the door and go to face them.

. . .

Megan and I go into the kitchen and Kathleen is here. She has her apron on, tied around her neck and her waist. She turns to us and her face lights up when she sees Megan.

"Beautiful girl," she says as she hugs her. "Did you have a good day?"

"I got chosen for the soccer team," Megan says proudly.

"My clever girl." Kathleen takes Megan's bag and coat from her and brushes past me as she goes to hang them in the hall.

I wait. I don't know why. It's the same every day. Every day, I wait and hope that it'll change, that she'll notice me. That I'll be beautiful enough for her to say hello to. And clever enough to get a hug.

"Tell me about it," she says to Megan, and she pulls out a chair so that her daughter can sit down. She pours her a glass of orange juice and passes her the bowl of yogurt and apple she's already prepared.

I walk back into the hallway and hang up my coat and bag. I take off my shoes and put them neatly on the mat before I go up the stairs.

One day, I'll shout and scream that I exist. One day, they'll know I'm here.

In my bedroom, the two chocolate muffins sit on my desk, as usual. I sit and eat, because if I throw them away, she'll know.

Maybe my dad will come back early. They'll cancel his night away and he'll be walking up our path in time for supper. I watch the gate through the window until my eyes start to blur. He's not here. He doesn't come.

So I curl up on my bed and wait.

. . .

"It's dinner time," Megan calls up the stairs.

I'm not hungry, but I know I have to go.

The smell of Kathleen's cooking comes up toward me and I push through it as I walk down.

In the kitchen, they're already sitting at the table. I look from one to the other, but they both ignore me as I sit down. Megan has an expression on her face that I can't read. They have bowls of freshly made stew in front of them. In my place, there's a plate of something different.

"Eat up, June," Kathleen smiles at me. She has that look in her eyes and now I can smell that she's given me dog food.

I look toward the door, but my dad is not there.

"I can't," I whisper.

"You will," Kathleen says.

They pick up their forks and begin to eat.

I sit as still as a stone. Maybe if I don't move, I'll disappear.

I can hear the sounds of their mouths chewing their food. Their forks scrape to pick up more mouthfuls.

Suddenly, Kathleen stands up. She grabs my hair and forces open my mouth.

"You will eat," she says, so quietly. "I've prepared this for you, so you will eat."

She shovels some onto a spoon and pulls my head back. I want to scream with the pain, but I have to keep my mouth shut.

The lumps of wet meat are at my lips and she's trying to force them in. No no no no no. *I'm stronger than you. I won't let you.*

"Megan, hold her nose." Kathleen sounds so calm, yet my head is ringing with terror.

Megan hesitates. It's enough to make Kathleen turn on her.

"Now," she says coldly.

Megan gets up. She squeezes my nostrils shut so tight that my eyes water.

And I have to breathe. I have no choice. The food meant for dogs is forced into my mouth. I gag at the feel of it. I don't want to swallow it, but my throat jolts and it slips down.

Kathleen spoons more in, until my mouth is full.

"You need some water," Megan says, and she lets go of my nose and grabs for a glass and there's water mixing with the dog food and spilling down my cheeks and squeezing down my throat. I'm thrashing out and Megan suddenly looks terrified. She knows I'm finding it hard to breathe.

"Mom," she says weakly.

Kathleen lets me go. My eyes are burning. My throat is numb.

I rush away from them, my school shirt wet, my mouth still full of the runny lumps.

I get to the bathroom before they can catch me and I put my fingers down my throat and retch and retch until my stomach is empty.

The smell of my vomit keeps filling the air.

AFTER

"But at what point is a child to blame?" Reverend Shaw asks.

"Megan knew what she was doing," I reply.

"Did she?" he asks gently. "I wonder really whether she knew. Or whether she had any control over it at all."

His words are taking me to a place I don't want to be, a time I don't want to remember. I don't want to think about how it could have been. I try instead to concentrate on the flowers that he's brought in from outside.

"I'm glad you're not choosing my wedding flowers," I say lightly.

"Church decoration isn't my strong point," he smiles. But he knows that I'm trying to take the conversation far away.

"People do strange things when they're scared," he tells me.

"Megan wasn't really scared."

"She was a child too," Reverend Shaw says. "A very lost one, I should imagine. You wouldn't have been the only person frightened of Kathleen. Any child living under her roof would have been terrified at times."

"So Megan could just do what she wanted? And get away with it all?"

"I'm not excusing her behavior," he says quickly. "But maybe now you can see it differently? Maybe you can distance yourself from the pain and try to see Megan for what she was—a confused child, just as scared as you, but in a different way."

I close my eyes as the sunlight streams in through the window. I need to think of something else. How these early spring days are my favorite, before it gets too hot and mosquitoes clam up the skies.

"June?" The reverend's voice is patient as he waits for me to open my eyes.

"But Megan hurt me." My tears are sudden and angry.

"I know."

"I don't feel sorry for her."

"I do," Reverend Shaw says calmly.

BEFORE
eleven years old

I decide to turn right outside the house and ride my bike along East Lane, even though there's never much to see this way. The freedom moves my legs, faster and faster. The fields are flat on either side of me and seem to stretch to the ends of the earth. I pass the Picketts' farm and, after longer still, the empty blue building I sometimes see from the car.

I pull my bike to a stop at the edge of Creeper's Forest. Dad's always made me promise never to go through it on my own, but, today, it doesn't seem frightening. I think it will curl around me and protect me from anything bad. I turn my wheels onto its path and start to move again.

The trees are packed tightly and almost block out the sunshine, but I'm not afraid. I like the way that the air is colder. I like the way it smells of dry sticks. It's bumpy, but if I follow the trees' lines, it's not too slow.

I'm humming to myself when I see light. I go toward it until I'm out of the forest, on a smaller track, but I'm not sure where it's going.

Further ahead, surrounded by more trees, there's a field of broken trailers. I slow down as I get closer. There are five of them, dotted around the edge of the small field. Weeds clamber up them and I can see that some have had their windows smashed. They have curved, soft roofs, covered with speckled moss and grime. But there's a path through the long grass, going from one to the other.

I lean my bike against the locked gate and look around. There's no one here, so I climb over and jump down the other side.

Slowly, I walk down the path to the nearest one. It smells rotten as I stand on my tiptoes and peer in the window. There's a kitchen, with a kettle and a bench and a table. It looks clean. Somebody has been here.

I walk carefully down the next path. The window of the second trailer is dirty, but I can see through it. There's no kitchen, just two small chairs and big cushions and piles of paper all over the floor. Hanging from the ceiling are tons of brightly colored shapes—bees and flowers and airplanes.

"Can I help you?" The voice startles me and I jump back.

"I was just looking," I say.

He's smaller than me, but not by much. His white cheeks are red from the sun and he has large freckles dotted over his nose. His glasses are too big.

"Why?" he asks.

"I saw the trailers."

"They're not mine," he says. "But I use them."

"Oh." I look back toward my bike. I can see its yellow handlebars sticking between the wood of the gate.

"Are you on your own?" the boy asks.

"Yes."

He looks at me, as though I'm meant to say something else.

"Did you make the paper shapes?" I ask, looking at them through the smeary window.

"Yes." He smiles and small dimples dent his cheeks.

"Can I see them?" I ask.

"OK," he nods.

He climbs up the steps of the trailer next to us and pushes open the door. I follow him up. Inside, the air is dry.

"This is my art room."

"Did you really make these?" I reach out gently to touch a paper Christmas tree that hangs from its star. It has so many layers and at the end of each branch sparkles a tiny bauble.

"Yup," he says proudly. "I'm Blister, by the way."

"Blister?" I smile cautiously.

"Long story."

"I've got lots of time."

"I was left out in the sun too long as a baby. Got burned so bad that I was one big blister. And the name stuck."

"That wasn't a long story."

"Nope, I suppose it wasn't," he laughs. "Do you want to see the other trailers?"

"OK."

He moves past me and we go down the steps, along the path and back toward the first trailer.

His T-shirt is too small. His trousers are too long.

He goes up the steps and moves back so that I can come in.

"Welcome to my kitchen," he says with a bow.

"It's lovely."

"Thank you. Do you want a drink?" He opens a cupboard and gets two glasses out. "You can have water, or water."

"I'll have water, then." I nearly laugh, but I don't.

He unscrews the lid of a big bottle, fills the glasses and passes one to me.

"What's your name?"

"June."

"That's a nice name."

"Thanks." I sip the water to stop a blush creeping up.

"Were you born in June?"

"Yes."

"It's the nicest month of the year, I reckon. Not too cold, not too boiling hot. In August, it's like an oven in here."

"Whose are these trailers, if they're not yours?"

"They were a man's, called Mr. Jones, but he killed his wife and then killed himself."

"He killed her?" I ask, looking around.

"It's all right," he laughs. "I don't think it was here. But their only child lives miles away and can't be bothered to keep the trailers properly, or sell the land. And no one else wants to come here—everyone says they're haunted."

"Are they?"

"I've never seen a ghost in them."

I follow him as he goes out and down the steps.

"So now they're all yours?" I ask as we walk back down the path.

"I pretend they are."

We go back into the trailer with all the shapes, and I copy Blister as he sits on a beanbag. He's a bit chubby, like me. His fingers are muddy and his nails are bitten down.

"I've been digging," he says.

I look away. "Oh."

"So, where do you live?" he asks, putting his glass down on the floor.

"Potter's Lane."

"Down by the river?"

"Yes," I say, my heart thumping a bit faster. "Where do you live?"

"Near Picker's Yard." He takes a piece of red paper from the table and starts to fold it.

"I don't know it," I say. Blister unfolds the paper and rubs it flat again.

"There's not much to know," he smiles. "But if you like chaos, you'd love my house. It's good chaos, though." He drinks a bit of his water. "Now, if this was orange juice, it would be delicious."

"It's still nice."

"Yeah, I suppose it is."

"How did he murder her?" I ask.

"Who?" He looks surprised.

"The husband. Who owned these trailers."

"Oh, right." Blister leans on his hands and stares at me across the table. His eyes are almost black, which looks a bit strange, as his skin is so rosy and white. "They say he strangled her and then chopped her up and . . ."

"No!" I laugh and put my hands over my ears. "I don't want to hear it."

Blister smiles at me. His dimples are on his cheeks again.

"Are you chicken?" he asks.

"No."

"I bet most of it's rumors."

"How long does it take you to do them?" I ask, looking up at the ceiling.

"My paper shapes?" We both stare at them, hanging like little planets. "Depends which one. That one—" Blister points to a seagull, flying silently above our head—"that didn't take long. But that one . . ." There's a castle, near the window.

"It's amazing."

"Yeah, I like it. That one took me a few hours. It took me ages just to get the turrets right."

"Can I touch it?"

"You'll see it better if you stand on a chair," Blister says, getting up.

I copy him, until I'm nose to nose with the castle walls.

"It's six pieces of paper, all stuck together, with thin cardboard for the floor," he says. When I touch the castle, it spins slightly. He's drawn a princess waving from one of the windows. "This is my best bit." Blister unhooks a thin piece of string and lowers the drawbridge. Inside is a little knight on a plastic horse, his sword pointing toward us.

"Did you really make the castle yourself?"

"It's not so hard." He draws the bridge up and gets down from his chair.

"I think it's really cool."

"Thanks." He moves the red piece of paper so that it meets the corner of the table. "I could teach you one day."

"Really?"

"Course." Blister rubs at the mud on the back of his hand. It changes to a light smudge.

"You don't go to my school," I say.

"I don't go to any school," he laughs.

"What do you mean?"

"Our mom and dad teach us at home."

"How?"

"They take turns, depending on if Dad's working."

"You really don't go to school?" A murmur of jealousy flickers inside me.

"No. We learn at home. Well, we try to. It's a bit chaotic at our house. I don't think they know where half of us are most of the time."

"Are there lots of you?"

"Seven—five boys and two girls. Nine, if you count Mom and Dad." He picks up a black crayon from the tub next to him and starts to draw a square in the middle of the red paper. "How many do you have?" He looks up. "Brothers and sisters?"

"One. Sort of," I say, but I don't want to. I don't want to think about Megan in here.

"How can you have a sort of? Are they cut in half?" Blister is drawing all sorts of thin lines in the middle of his square.

"She's a stepsister."

"Oh, one of those." He swaps the crayon for a pencil. "It must be quite nice, just having one."

"I guess."

"Most of mine are adopted. Mom and Dad had Maggie and me, but then they couldn't have any more, so they adopted lots instead. It's good, though."

I watch him draw and rub at the lines. His eyes screw up a little bit, in concentration. He scratches his shoulder, before he picks up the paper and shows it to me.

"What do you think?"

I think it's meant to be the skull of some sort of animal.

"It's good," I say, although I'm not really sure it is. But I like the way that he took his time drawing it, how careful he was.

"You can have it, if you want." Blister folds it in half and then half again and passes it to me.

"Thanks," I say.

"So, if you have a stepsister, does that mean you live with your mom or dad?" he asks, sipping at his water again.

"My dad."

"Where's your mom?"

"She's dead," I say. The word hangs between us, then drifts up to the colored shapes above our heads.

"Do you miss her?" Blister asks quietly.

"Yes."

He nods his head, as though he knows.

"Do you want more water?"

"No. I should be getting back."

"Will you come here again?"

I stand up and put my skull picture in the back pocket of my shorts.

"Yes," I say, and he smiles. No one ever smiles because of me. Well, only my dad and Jennifer. It feels like the sunshine is actually in the trailer. "I like it here." I smile back at him.

Blister stays on the steps of the trailer and watches me clamber over the gate. When I look back, he salutes me and I wave at him before I pedal off quickly.

The wind is warm on my face as I rush back through the forest.

Blister is my friend. Blister is my friend.

I know I won't tell a soul. I'll hide my piece of red paper and keep the secret of him tucked so close that no one will ever know.

. . .

"Come in," Mr. Cleadon says, standing up from behind his desk. "Do take a seat."

"Thank you," Kathleen says. She lets go of my hand briefly, as we sit down, but then she picks it up again.

"I'm sorry to have to call you in, Mrs. Kingston."

"That's fine." Kathleen smiles at him and then at me.

"I'm not sure if June has told you what this is about?"

"No." She looks straight at my headmaster. Her clogged eyes don't blink.

"Right. Well. June has been caught stealing," Mr. Cleadon says. I breathe in sharply and feel Kathleen tense beside me. I think Mr. Cleadon expects her to say something, but there's only silence and the ticking of the clock on the shelf in the corner. "Unfortunately, some money and possessions went missing and they were found in June's bag and desk."

"It wasn't me," I say quietly.

Mr. Cleadon puffs the air in his cheeks. "We've been through this, June."

There's no point in me saying any more. I've tried telling him the truth, but he won't believe anything I say.

"Are you sure about this?" Kathleen asks. She reaches over and tucks a curl behind my ear. I try not to flinch. "June is such a good girl. I find it hard to believe that she would do that."

"Some children saw her do it."

Kathleen shakes her head. "It's been a difficult time for June," she says. She looks so like she cares that I almost believe her. "You know that she lost her mother a few years ago."

"I'm fully aware of that, Mrs. Kingston. But stealing is something we can't excuse."

"No, of course not. And I'm sure that June is sorry. It's just that there are special circumstances here."

"I know. Which is why, because this is the first time, the punishment in school will be minimal. And I hope that at home you'll make it clear to her that stealing is just unacceptable."

"Of course. June knows that it's wrong. You have my word that it won't happen again."

"Try to keep out of trouble, June," Mr. Cleadon says with a smile that barely reaches his mouth, let alone his eyes.

We get up to leave and Kathleen kisses the top of my head.

"It'll be OK," she says, as she takes my hand and leads me from the room.

• • •

We sit through supper and I'm waiting. Slowly, I eat the pile of food in front of me. I don't look up once.

Megan is telling Kathleen about her day, about the volcano they're making as a class and how she's in charge of the flames. She's going to cover cardboard with bright tissue paper and stick it jagged from the top.

The brownie is sickly sweet and I force spoonful after spoonful of it down. The sponge is sprinkled thick with sugar and sits heavy on my teeth. I scrape my plate, until every last drop is gone.

"So, you're a thief as well." Kathleen's words are for me. I don't want them, but that doesn't stop them. "I bet your mom was a thief, too. Nasty little woman that she was."

Anger bubbles in me. It takes over my bones and I have to clasp the sides of my chair to stop myself from screaming.

"Like mother, like daughter, and we can't be having that."

Kathleen stands up and walks out of the room. I see her going across the hallway and into the living room.

"You're at the bottom of the heap," Megan says. "And your mom was ugly too."

It's too late to stop myself. I jump up so quickly that Megan's eyes flash with fear and I'm on her, pulling her hair and thumping her with my tight fists.

"She wasn't, she wasn't, she wasn't." I don't care that I'm crying. And I don't care that Megan is curled up, screaming on the floor.

I hear the front door opening, but I carry on.

"June!" my dad shouts. He pulls me from her, just as Kathleen comes back in. She has her sewing basket in her hand.

"Megan!" she exclaims as she drops the basket and scoops her daughter up.

"What's going on?" my dad asks. He's holding me at arm's length.

I'm breathing hard. I've never laid a finger on Megan before. But, today, fire got into me. I stare back at my dad, bewildered by what I've just done.

"I came back early to surprise you," he says, and he looks so confused.

"I'm sorry," I tell him. And I am, because I've made him look sad.

"Why did you do it?"

"It was just a silly quarrel, Bradley. Don't be hard on her," Kathleen says, putting her hand softly on his arm. "It's over now."

Megan is still crying slightly. It's strange to see her curled up there.

"Fine," my dad says. "But you're to go to your room, June.

And if I ever see you hurting Megan again, there'll be hell to pay. Do you understand?"

I nod and run away, leaving them huddled together on the kitchen floor.

. . .

The next day after school, I know I can't stay in the house. I put a note on the kitchen table—*"I'm going to Jennifer's. Back later."* And then I leave it all behind me, the wind rushing past my ears.

I can hear Blister humming to himself from the edge of the path. He's sitting on the trailer steps and he sees me as I start to climb over the gate. In his hand is a little penknife and it points straight to the sky as he waves.

He grins at me. "You came back." He puts down the stick that he's carving and walks through the grassy path.

"I hoped you'd be here," I say, wriggling my arms to get the bag off my back. "I brought you something." He watches me as I unzip it and pull out the small bottle of orange juice. "I thought you'd like this," I say. Suddenly, it seems a bit strange. It felt like a good idea earlier, but now I feel awkward as I give it to him. "You said orange juice would be better."

He looks up at me as if I've given him a bar of gold.

"Thanks, June," he says. I follow him back to the steps. "Look what I did." He picks up the stick he's been carving. It's a small spear, with a sharp, pointed end. "To keep the ghosts away," he laughs, and throws it straight into the ground, where it stays, sticking upright. "Nothing will get past that."

We go into the trailer and I watch as he pours the orange juice into two glasses.

"Presto," he says, and clinks my glass.

"Presto," I say, as though it's our own secret code, the key to our club.

"Shall we drink it in the art room?" Blister asks. Before I even nod, he's off and I'm following him, looking at the muddy streak stretched straight across his arm.

"After you." He bows deeply, one arm swept to the side, the other tilting too much and spilling juice on the steps.

"Why thank you, sir." And I climb up into the second trailer. The smell of glue mixes into the warmth, and I notice that the piles of paper on the floor are stacked with their colors in order.

"You're very tidy."

"It's how I like it."

"Maybe because your home is so busy?" I say.

Blister rubs his cheek. "Maybe. I hadn't thought of that."

We put our glasses next to the cushions. Blister kneels down, picks up a piece of paper from each pile and lays them out in the middle of the floor.

"So, what do you want to make?" he asks. I stretch my legs out straight and wriggle my toes in my sandals.

"I don't know," I say.

Blister crawls over to a tiny table and picks up a tube of glue. I watch as he takes one piece of white paper and one piece of gold. He starts to fold them and it's as if I disappear. He screws up his nose slightly as he concentrates and it squashes some of his freckles.

His fingers move carefully. He folds and twists and sticks the paper, as though it's a precious jewel. I'm not really thinking about the shape—I just like watching something beautiful appear out of something so ordinary.

44

It's finished and Blister holds it up in front of him.

"It's an angel. For your mom," he says.

I reach out to touch her wings and the clothes of white and gold. Her face is blank, but I know she's happy.

"I didn't want to make you sad," Blister says.

"I'm not," I say quietly. But I am. I'm so sad that I don't know how my heart carries on beating.

Blister puts the angel in my hands. I want her to be big, so I can hug her.

"Was your mom nice?" Blister asks.

"Yes," I say, and I pull my knees up tight into my chest and look down, so he can't see my eyes.

"I don't mind if you cry," he says. He puts his hand on my shoulder. "It's not fair that she died."

But I press my head into my knees, until I know the tears have stopped.

When I look up, Blister is sitting with a little rag in his hand.

"It's the cleanest I've got," he says.

I take it from him. It feels rough against my eyes, but I don't mind.

"Thanks," I say.

A silence now sits between us and I don't know how to fill it.

"What's your stepmother like?" Blister finally asks.

"She's OK," I lie, holding my angel tightly. Blister looks at me as though I should say some more. "I'd better go. She'll be worried about where I am."

"Oh."

"Sorry. I'll come again, I promise." I stand up and Blister gets up too.

"Can I keep my angel?" I ask.

"Of course. I made her for you." Blister smiles and his dimples dip in. He pushes his glasses up a bit on his nose.

"Thanks," I say.

I put her carefully into my bag, worried that I might hurt her. I don't want her to get crumpled. I want to get her to the house safely, where I'll tuck her away in a secret box.

My very own angel.

AFTER

Mickey and I walk side by side. The sun is warm on my face and there's not a cloud in the sky.

"Where shall we go today?" I ask.

"The fields at the back of my house?" she replies.

"I'd like that."

We walk slowly—Mickey's hip makes her seem older than she is. She shuffles slightly, the dry dust lifting around her ankles.

High above us, two birds swoop and twist before they disappear from view.

"Birds are like memories," I say. Mickey chuckles. She's used to my thoughts by now. "They are," I insist. "How sometimes they're close enough to see clearly, but at other times they fly just out of reach."

"You've been reading too many books again."

"I can't work out whether memories are good or bad," I say.

"I suppose it depends which ones they are." Mickey sounds

tired now. "Maybe you should try to remember the good and forget the bad."

"But sometimes even the good ones hurt," I tell her.

Mickey nods as she puts her hand gently on my arm.

"Let's make happy memories for today, then," she smiles.

"How?"

"You see those horses over there?" She points into the distance. At first they're difficult to see, but then the herd of them becomes clearer. "How about we go and ride them?"

"They're not ours," I laugh.

"They could be if we take them." Mickey is laughing so hard that we have to stop walking. She leans into me as she starts to cough, but they're happy tears in her eyes.

And I laugh with her too, the sound sweeping up to the wide blue above us.

"It's good to be alive," she says. But this time the coughing pulls at her body and I know she's hurting. "Let's go back, June," she says.

BEFORE

twelve years old

"You're worth a million of those kids from school, June," Blister tells me.

"I'm not."

"You are." He pokes a tiny stick into the braces stuck like train tracks on his teeth.

The grass is warm and prickly under my stomach. Our field feels like an oven, but it's better than the cold in winter, when Blister and I wrap up in virtually all the clothes we own, but it's still so freezing in our trailers that we can barely move.

"I don't know how you do it every day." Blister has his angry face back and I know that beneath his lips, his teeth are clamped tightly shut. His eyes look fiery.

"I just do."

"But you shouldn't have to."

"I have to go to school. And it's not so bad." I shrug.

"It is. And you know it. It's not right that some human beings treat others like that. What gives them the right?"

"They seem to like it."

"I bet they don't. I bet when they're at home on their own they feel terrible about themselves."

"Do you think?" I ask.

"It's impossible to be so mean to someone and not feel bad somewhere. Deep down, right inside them, I bet they wish they didn't do it."

"Even Ryan?"

"Even Ryan."

"And Cherry?"

"Yes. And Lauren. And they better watch out, because karma will be waiting for them."

"Who's Karma?"

"My mom told me about it." Blister sits up and crosses his legs. The anger has left him and his face looks serious. "She says that the bad things you do will always come back to you. Even if it's years in the future. That's why you've got to be nice."

I think of karma, waiting like a black shadow for Kathleen. I imagine it just around the corner, sharpening its nails.

"Will it come to Kathleen and Megan?" I ask Blister. He looks up at me quickly.

"Are they being horrible to you again?"

"A bit," I say.

"What are they doing?" I know he cares, that he really wants to know, but I don't want to bring their badness here now.

"They just say nasty things," I say.

"Then they'll pay too, June."

And it makes me feel good. Because I've got someone else on my side.

"Karma is powerful stuff," he says.

"I wish I could keep it in a bottle and use it when I need it," I say.

Blister laughs. "Don't worry. It'll be there."

I look up at the bright blue sky.

You won't catch me, Karma, I think. *I won't do anything bad.*

And I close my eyes and breathe in the dry smell of our field and the muddy smell of Blister and I know that I'm happy.

"Do you reckon the rabbit has been buried long enough?" Blister asks. I open my eyes and sit up to face him.

"How long's it been?"

"Three months," he says. Three months since we found the rabbit dead in the forest, when we'd buried it properly and I'd said a prayer.

"Is that enough time?" I ask.

"It normally is."

Blister stands up quickly. He's always the most excited about this bit, as though he's digging up treasure. He doesn't like to leave the animals alone in the ground, when he can find them and make them beautiful again.

We walk quickly through the grass and Blister goes into our Bones Trailer to get a bag and two trowels. He passes one to me and we climb through the fence at the back of our field and into the cool of our forest.

We follow the path in silence. Blister likes this bit to be quite solemn. Out of respect, he says.

It isn't difficult to find the little cross. He always buries the animals in the same place. If there's more than one at a time, he buries them side by side.

"Are you sure it's been long enough?" I ask as we start to dig. I don't want it to be like the last time, when there were sticky tendons still stuck to the bird's bones.

"I think so," Blister says, and he picks up the earth in his trowel and trickles it gently next to us. "Be careful," he reminds me.

We dig more slowly as we get deeper.

I see it first, a dusty white color sticking up through the brown.

"Stop," I say, and push Blister's arm away from the hole. I press my fingers into the earth and gently pry the first bone loose.

"Wow, that's a beauty," Blister says, and I smile with pride, as though this is all my work. He unzips the bag and I place the bone gently inside.

Blister pushes the crumbled earth aside until he reaches the next one. He rubs it slightly and pushes up his glasses with his muddy finger.

"Tibia, I reckon," he says.

"Is that the leg bone?" I ask, and he nods his head.

I let him dig with his fingers until he finds the skull. He cups it in both his hands and holds it up.

"Look at that," he says. I nod and try not to think of my mom.

We collect the rest of the bones and when we're sure we've got them all, we push the earth back into its hole and I flatten the top with the palm of my hand. Blister puts the little cross at the top of his bag and we walk in silence back to our trailers.

. . .

"Blister, do you think I'm fat?"

He's laying the rabbit bones out on the table in height order. They're washed clean and he's dried each one of them carefully. He stops what he's doing and looks at me.

"A bit," he says. "Do you think I am?"

"A bit," I say, and smile, but inside, my heart is hammering, because I know I'm going to tell him.

"What?" he says, laughing as I stare at him.

"Kathleen makes me eat too much," I say quickly. "She wants me to be fat."

I don't know what I expect him to say. I don't even know if I want him to say anything. Maybe I should try to swallow the words right back up and we can both forget that they ever hung in the air.

"Does she do it to Megan?" he asks quietly.

"No. She gives her a little. She gives me a lot."

"I thought she just said nasty things to you," he says.

"And this as well," I say, and hold my breath.

"Can you ask her not to?" he asks.

It feels like the world is beginning to crumble under me.

"It doesn't matter," I say. I want to look at him and smile. To pretend that I haven't wanted to tell him for forever and now his answer is all wrong.

Blister shivers, as if he's cold, and starts to rearrange the rabbit shapes slightly. I know I can't let Kathleen darken his life too.

"What are we doing with these?" I ask, pushing her far away from here.

"I want to give this to Tom for his birthday," he says. "Do you want to hold, or glue?"

"I'll glue," I say.

Blister picks up two bones. "Just here," he says, and points clumsily with his thumb.

I squirt some glue onto the plate, dip in the plastic brush and sweep it over the hard top of the rabbit's leg. Blister pushes it into the femur.

"I'll hold too," I say as I put the glue on the other leg. "What happened to your glasses?" There's sticky tape wrapped around the arm and rim, and it makes them slant slightly.

"Eddie sat on them."

"Does it make everything wobbly?"

"It's fine," he says, scrunching up his nose. "Do you know what my favorite color is today?"

"Green?"

"No."

"Black?"

"Nope. Orange. I love that color."

"Today, mine's turquoise," I say.

"Turquoise?"

"It's pretty," I say.

"Like you," Blister smiles. He'll look strange when the train tracks are taken off and all his toothy gaps have gone.

"Like you too," I say.

"Can I be handsome instead?"

"You can be that too."

Blister moves his hand very slowly from the rabbit's leg. The bone holds.

"Ta-da," he says proudly, but the bone slips down and crashes to the table. "Tom better appreciate this," he mumbles, pushing the bone back into place. "It's going to take us forever."

"I've got forever," I say.

The skull is the difficult part. Blister puts a stick through the holes, to help it stay in place. We take turns holding it.

"Are you going to paint it?" I ask, my arms beginning to ache a bit.

"I might. Maybe black?" Blister thinks. Black bones. I wonder if anyone has ever had black bones.

"Tom'd like that," I say. He hands the small skeleton to me. It feels heavy, but I know it's not. I imagine it with fur, with eyes looking at me. With a little heart beating and blood being where it's meant to be. Instead of this, all gone.

"Blister?" I ask.

"Mm." He's looking in the cupboard. There's a small line of his skin showing under his T-shirt as he reaches up.

"What do you think happens to us when we die?"

He puts a tub of black paint on the table, but then he stops and looks at me.

"Do you think there's a heaven?" I ask.

"I know there is," he says. He's so sure. "Otherwise, what would be the point?"

"To life?"

"Yeah. And it wouldn't be fair, otherwise. Some people die as babies, others live to a hundred. It wouldn't be fair if that was it. You've got to have somewhere to go on to."

"Is my mom there?"

"Definitely," Blister says.

He gets up to pick a paintbrush from the bucket and scoops a mug of water from the bowl. He has to work the spoon all the way round the lid of the paint tin until it gives way and lifts off.

"Will the black stay on?" I ask.

"I think I'll have to go over it a few times."

The smell of paint fills the trailer, even with the door hooked open.

"Do you ever go to church?" I ask him.

"Only at Thanksgiving and Christmas. Mom finds it a bit stressful, though, with half of us crawling around the floor, the other half laughing in the wrong bits."

"I don't find it stressful. I like it."

"I didn't know you went."

"I used to, sometimes. With my mom. We'd dress up a bit and go to the church over near Neville's Creek. We'd drive there together, just me and her." It felt like the sun was always shining on those days. Mom would hold my hand and we'd sing so our songs wove in and out of the rafters.

"How come she drowned, June?" Blister doesn't look at me as he speaks. Instead, he concentrates on making the white bones black. I move my fingers slightly so they don't get covered in paint. "You don't have to say."

"It's OK," I tell him, although it's not. "It was the river by our house. She went for a swim and got caught in the weeds."

Blister sucks the air in through his teeth.

"That's horrible," he says.

"I think she must have been frightened," I say quietly. It's difficult to get the words out. I've thought them so many times, but I've never actually said it. Blister puts the paintbrush down.

"Yes. She would have been. But only for a bit, June. I've read that it's a peaceful way to die."

I can't answer him. Nothing makes it better.

"I wish it hadn't happened to you," Blister says. I nod and touch the wet paint gently with my fingertips. It's darker than my skin. I hold the bones still and wait for it to dry.

• • •

I'm happy when I walk into our house. I've gotten better at keeping hold of my good times with Blister and carrying them with me through the front door.

But Kathleen grabs me. She yanks my ribbon from my hair. Terror swoops into me as she drags me into the kitchen, where Megan stands silently in the corner.

Kathleen holds my arms tight by my side as she pushes me into a chair. She's somehow managed to grab my head too and she tips it back, forcing my mouth open wide.

"Quickly," she says. I can't see Megan now, but I can hear her scuttling closer.

Megan's face is expressionless as she lowers my red ribbon until it sits at the back of my throat. I start to gag, but it only makes it go down further.

"Twist it around," Kathleen tells her. Megan looks at her, as though she doesn't understand. But when Kathleen nods she slowly begins to turn the ribbon stuck in my throat. I writhe to get away, but Kathleen is too strong. She's always too strong.

"Put your hand over her mouth," Kathleen tells her. Megan pauses. Fear creeps into her eyes. "Do it now," Kathleen says. Megan's hand feels small and she doesn't press down hard, but my throat tightens and I retch.

I can't breathe.

I'm going to die.

I'm coughing and the ribbon is sticking and building in my throat. I know Kathleen is laughing, but all I can hear is the blood thumping in my ears and my legs stamping on the floor.

My dad will come back and then he'll know. I'll lie bloated on his kitchen floor and they won't escape this time.

Megan lets go of my mouth and backs away as I gasp for air, but the ribbon sticks so far down my throat that I can't stop myself vomiting. Kathleen holds my head back tight and the vomit is gurgling like lumps of acid.

My dad will find me too late.

She throws my head forward and I'm sick all over my lap. I'm breathing so hard, trying to get enough air into me. Trying not to die.

"You're disgusting, just like your mom," I hear Kathleen say. "Clean up this mess. I don't want black girl's vomit on my floor."

. . .

In my bedroom, I can still smell the sharp smell. I've washed my clothes in the bathtub and scrubbed my hands, but it seems to have found a way into me and I can't get it out.

Quietly, I open my bottom drawer. I take out the top two sweaters and find my shoebox underneath. I lift it out, put it on the floor in front of me and take off the lid.

All my most precious things fill it. Memories of my mom, and Blister's paper shapes. I find my white angel and hold her to me. She'll be able to hear my heartbeat. She lets me cry, quietly, so they can't hear.

The pain of needing my mom is like burning coal inside me. I want her to come back. I want her here, in my bedroom now, holding my hand and braiding my hair.

I'm crushing my angel too tight. I don't want to damage her. She tells me to cry until there's nothing left and the feeling in my chest becomes more like an ache.

Carefully, I put her back among my paper castle and my tulip and all the other things that Blister's made for me. I put the lid back on, to keep them safe, put the box back in the drawer with the sweaters on top and silently push the drawer closed.

. . .

Miss Sykes touches my arm as I'm about to walk out of the classroom the next day.

"June, can I have a word?" she asks.

I stand by her desk and watch the rest of the children go. Miss Sykes sits down and takes off her half-moon glasses. They hang from blue string around her neck.

"Is everything all right with you at the moment, June?"

"Yes, Miss Sykes."

"Are any of the children still upsetting you?"

I look at the floor. "No, Miss Sykes."

"I heard Kelly making a jibe about your weight," she says. I bite the inside of my cheek.

"It's not bad," I say.

"Any name-calling is bad."

I look up at the clock and then at the door.

"And how about at home? Is everything all right at home?" I stare at her. Is this a trap? Is Kathleen hiding somewhere, ready to pounce? "June?"

"I'm going to be late for lunch, Miss Sykes," I say.

She looks at me and sighs deeply. "All right, but promise me you'll talk to me if you need to."

I nod. But I know she'd never believe me. They never do. And before she can ask any more I'm gone.

. . .

It's been a week since Blister and I made Tom's birthday present and the rain soaks me as I pedal fast to his house. I'm wearing my raincoat, so my arms and back are dry, but my legs are shiny with wet. The hood keeps my hair dry, but it can't keep the rain out of my eyes.

The path leading up to their house is always littered with things that should be inside. Clothes, or a chair, or a boot. They're like secret signs to follow, to get to the front door. Someone must pick them up eventually, as they change every time.

Today, there's a sweater left in the rain. A bit further on, there's a toy oven, puddles gathering on the plastic. A teddy bear lies face down in the water.

I leave my bike leaning against the hedge and go up the path. I don't knock on their front door. No one would answer in any case.

The door handle is dented and I don't even have to turn it. I just push the door open and poke my head around. There's no one here.

"Hello?" I call. There are sounds coming from all over the house.

Mr. Wick walks out of the kitchen, a dishcloth slung over his shoulder, icing on his chin.

"June!" he says. He comes over and hugs me, even though I'm soaking wet. He smells of flour and wood-chips. "Blister!" he yells up the stairs. He looks back at me. "Come in and close the door."

I shut the rain out, but I know it'll take ages for my shoes to dry.

"I'll put your raincoat by the stove," Mr. Wick says. I'm dripping all over his floor, but he doesn't seem to notice. "Blister!" He leaves me standing in the hall as he disappears into the kitchen.

"Hi, June," Mrs. Wick calls from the kitchen. I go through

the big, white door, to find her stacking cookies onto a plate. She stops what she's doing, just to come to see me.

"Your hair looks lovely like that," she tells me, and she kisses me once on one cheek and once on the other. I spent a long time deciding on my hair this morning and it's in two buns, high up on my head. "Come and stand where it's warm."

She's fussing me over to the stove when Blister comes in.

"Hiya," he says. He's always a bit different with me when we're here, as though we need our trailers to really be us. He reaches out for a cookie.

"Uh-uh," Mrs. Wick says, and swipes his hand away.

"Have you given Tom his present?" I ask him.

"Not yet. I was waiting for you to get here."

He disappears into the room next door and comes back with a package wrapped in newspaper. It's covered in tiny paper ladybugs.

"Where is he, Mom?"

"He could be anywhere," she laughs, filling a jug of water.

Blister sticks his head out the kitchen door.

"Tom!" he yells.

"You could try looking," Mr. Wick says as he rinses the empty sieve.

"Come on," Blister says to me.

We find Tom in the study with Mil. Blankets drape across their dad's desk and hang down either side. We can hear them, chattering away from inside.

"Can we come in?" Blister asks.

"Password?" Tom asks.

"Horse."

"No."

"Feet?"

"Nope," Mil giggles.

"Well, if you don't want your present," Blister laughs and stomps loudly back to the door.

The blanket whips aside.

"June!" Mil smiles at me. She has a streak of jam across her cheek.

"You can come in," Tom says. So I wriggle in beside them, pushing the plate of half-eaten sandwiches out of the way.

"How does it feel to be six?" I ask.

"Good," Tom says, smiling, although his breath is wheezy.

"How are you feeling?"

"OK."

"Blister says the new medicine is yuck," I say. Tom nods his head and screws up his nose.

Blister comes in and pulls the blanket closed behind him. It's darker, but not pitch black. Light scoots in around the edges.

"This is for you." Blister passes the present to Tom. "It's from me and June."

Tom smiles. "Thanks." He picks off every one of the lady-bugs and lines them up in a row at the edge of the hideout.

"Careful opening it," Blister tells him.

Tom rips back the newspaper, until he's holding the rabbit's black skeleton. Even in the dim light, I can see happiness in his eyes.

"Wow," he says.

"We spent ages making it," Blister says, and I think of the furry animal I laid in the hole, all those months ago.

"Thanks," Tom says. "I love it. Thanks, June." His big smile has his top two teeth missing.

"You're welcome," I say, hugging him.

And I wish we could all stay in here forever.

．．．

I've never sat with Blister's whole family at the table before. Blister says it doesn't happen often, because no one is ever completely sure where everyone else is.

We somehow fit. Eddie sits on an old oil drum, Chubbers is in the high chair and the rest of us have managed to find a chair from those scattered around the house.

Tom has a paper crown pushed tight upon his head and Maggie sits grumpy at the edge of the table.

She never says much to me, but I wish she was my sister. She'd do my hair and teach me about make-up. Even though my skin is a different color than hers, she'd experiment with what looked best and find colors that suited me. She'd tell me I look pretty and that she's proud I'm her sister.

Eddie is yelling and Mr. Wick is bellowing at him to be quiet. Chubbers throws his food on the floor and Mil is crying because of something Eddie said, but Tom sits happily, sucking his drink loudly through a straw.

I look at Mrs. Wick and for the first time I see how tired she is.

"How are your parents?" she asks me when she sees me watching her.

"My dad's fine," I say. "He's very busy." Too busy to notice. Too busy to save me.

"And Megan must be nine, or ten now?"

"She's just eleven," I say.

She raises her eyebrows. "Where does the time go?"

"No, Chubs!" Maggie shouts at the baby. He looks at her in surprise and I watch as his face screws up slowly, turning from white to red. He can yell like no one else.

Si screams and covers his ears.

"Enough," Mrs. Wick says. Her dress looks heavy as she gets up, weighing down her shoulders. She takes the shrieking Chubbers out of his high chair and he jerks his legs straight as she cuddles him into her neck.

Blister looks at Tom, who's still sitting beaming in his crooked paper hat.

"Happy birthday," he laughs.

Maggie gets up and marches out of the room, slamming the door behind her.

• • •

I have to leave Tom's birthday early to get home in time for supper. My dad insists that Saturday evening is the one meal every week we all eat together.

"A bit less for June," I hear him say quietly to Kathleen as she piles up my plate.

"She likes it like this, Bradley," she replies in an over-emphasized whisper.

Liar, I want to say to her.

"She needs to cut back a bit," my dad says, as though I can't hear. As though I'm not in the room.

"OK." Kathleen takes a spoonful of mashed potatoes away. She puts the plate in front of me on the table and in full view of my dad she cuts some butter and drops it on the top, where it instantly starts to melt. She looks at me with a smile that says to Dad that she's on my side. That she did it because she loves me.

I want to take the boiling potatoes and throw them at her.

"You OK, honey?" She reaches over and pats my hand.

"Yes," I say, and pick up my fork and begin to eat.

"How was Jennifer today, June?" my dad asks.

"She's good," I lie.

"You should invite her over here again one day. You don't always have to go there."

"She's teaching me violin," I lie again. "It's not so easy for her to bring it here."

"We'll have to come over one day and hear a recital," Kathleen says.

"I bet you're really good." Megan smiles at me.

Can't you see? I want to scream at my dad. *How can you not see that they hate me?*

I eat my food slowly.

"Dad's teaching me how to make shelves," Megan says. I hate it when she calls him Dad. I stare hard at her and she knows what I'm thinking. *He's my dad, not yours. He'll never be yours.* Her smile doesn't waver. "We cut the wood to size today and started to plane it."

"You're a great little apprentice," my dad says. And he nods his head, as he eats another mouthful. "You should join us one day, June."

"Maybe," I say. I look away from him and put my fork into the mound of food on my plate.

. . .

There's a knock on my bedroom door. My dad peers his head around.

"Can I come in?"

I put my book down and move over on my bed to make space. He closes the door behind him.

"What are you reading?" he asks. The mattress squeaks under the weight of him.

"It's a Judy Blume." I put it face down so he can't read the cover.

"Pumpkin," he says heavily, "you've got to make a bit more of an effort with Megan."

His feet are squarely on the floor and he has to twist slightly to look at me. "All she wants is a sister. Can't you see how desperate she is for the two of you to get along?"

"No," I say. Suddenly it feels like there's not enough air in the room. I want to get up and open the window, but I'm scared I'll crack apart piece by piece if I even move.

"We're so lucky to have them, June. You might not feel it now, but when you're older I promise you'll realize it."

"What was wrong with it being just you and me?" I ask. My head is bent so far forward that there's no chance of him looking into my eyes. I don't want him to see how close I am to crying.

"I was lonely, June. Weren't you?"

"No. I had you."

"I fell in love with Kath. And it's like she saved me. She gave me a reason to smile again."

Wasn't I a good enough reason?

I push my fingers hard into my palms.

"Sometimes, she's not very nice to me," I blurt out. My heart is hammering so hard that it hurts my skin.

"Oh, Pumpkin. She can't be nice all the time."

"She's never nice." I'm trying so hard not to cry. I need to keep my voice clear, so that he can understand.

"You know that's not true." I can tell he's losing patience with me. "You've just got to start being fairer to her. I know she's not your mom and I know that must really hurt, but if you want to love Kath, your mom would understand. She'd be so happy that you've got another mom who loves you."

He won't hear me and my tears tip out. I pull my knees up tight to my face to make myself into a ball small enough to disappear.

"Honey," my dad says. And he puts his arms around me and rocks me as though I'm a child again. I imagine my mom here, hugging me too. The sharp smell of coffee. The warm feel of her skin. And her soft voice singing to me and telling me I'm her beautiful little girl.

My tears soak my knees. And they don't make me feel any better.

AFTER

"My dad just wouldn't see," I tell Reverend Shaw. Today, I feel angry and I hope he can unwind the thread of red that's twisting inside me. "Or maybe he just didn't want to."

"Sometimes, people are blind to what's right in front of them," he says calmly.

"He cared more for Kathleen than me. That's why he didn't want to open his eyes."

"I could probably swear on this Bible that's not true," Reverend Shaw says. "You can love someone deeply, but somehow not always do the right thing by them. People have flaws. We get so much wrong. Maybe if you try to understand him as a human being with faults, then you can move forward."

"But he could have stopped it."

"He couldn't stop something that he didn't know existed."

"You sound like you're excusing him," I say.

"I'm not. I'm just suggesting that you forgive him."

"It's not that simple," I tell him.

"Isn't it?" the reverend asks. "If I gave you the choice of two paths, which would you take—the one filled with brambles and fog, or the clear one?"

"You know which one," I say.

"It's your choice, June. It's your life and you get to choose your path. Carry your past down the difficult route, or take your past from your shoulders, leave it here and walk down the other road."

"You make it seem easy," I tell him.

"Perhaps it is," he replies.

BEFORE
thirteen years old

Jennifer stretches her legs out in front of her, two white sticks, side by side. She points her toes hard at the end. I have to shuffle down the wall slightly as she raises her arms in a circle around her head, her fingers barely touching at the top.

"Mom says that if I don't practice more I'll have to give up lessons," she says.

"You've asked for pointe shoes for your birthday, though."

"I know. That's why I've got to keep practicing," she says.

"Wouldn't it be easier to be standing up?" I suggest.

"Maybe." She slides her foot up her leg.

"You've made a triangle," I say.

"It's called a passé," she says, although I can tell that she's finding it difficult to get it right, sitting like this.

There's laughter close by in the playground. I look up to see a knot of girls over by the wire fence, with Megan in the middle of them. She's got that smile that isn't a real one. The one she wears to school ever since Anne said they weren't friends anymore.

She doesn't see me watching. Anne grabs Megan's bag, opens it and starts throwing things on the floor.

"Is that your Megan?" Jennifer asks, lowering her hands onto the brick wall. *She's not* my *Megan.*

"Yes." There's fear in Megan's eyes and it sits strangely in my stomach. Anne is looking for something, but I don't think she finds it. Instead, she throws Megan's bag high into the air for another girl to catch.

"Should you help her?" Jennifer asks.

No.

I get up. I don't want to, but I'm walking toward them. Megan sees me. There are so many jumbled words and complicated thoughts between her eyes and mine.

Anne throws the bag high and I'm almost there, but the bell clangs and the girls quickly scatter.

Megan is left on her own, picking up her things from the scuffed ground. She doesn't look at me again. But I can tell that underneath her red cheeks she's clamping her teeth tight to stop the tears from squeezing through.

"We should help her," Jennifer whispers from next to me.

"We'll be late for class," I say. And I turn, with my head held high, and walk steadily back across the emptying playground, toward the heavy school door.

. . .

"How was school?" Kathleen asks. I know the question isn't for me, so I won't bother trying to reply. One day, I might. One day, I'll answer and watch the confusion on Kathleen's face, as she has to realize I'm really here.

"Fine," Megan says. She's lying, so she keeps her eyes from looking at mine.

"I thought we'd go shopping on Saturday, to choose Anne's present," Kathleen says. Panic flares in Megan's eyes. *She's not invited anymore*, I want to say.

"OK," Megan says, her voice sounding tiny.

"We could get you a nice new pair of jeans, too, while we're there."

I poke my fork into the peas on my plate. Four fit on one tine, but the fifth is too difficult and it gets squashed. I pull them off with my teeth, so that they drop one at a time onto my tongue.

"Bigger mouthfuls, June," Kathleen says.

I pierce the fork into the sausage and I stare at her as I force the whole thing into my mouth. She's not looking at me, but she knows.

She takes her napkin from her lap and dabs it at the corner of her mouth. A little bit of pink lipstick smudges onto the material before she folds it into a square and puts it on the table.

I'm trying to chew as her chair scrapes backwards. Megan is looking down. I'm glad that neither of them can see my heart. It's beating so quickly that it'd give my fear away.

Kathleen grabs my plate. She yanks my arm and pulls me under the table. I watch as she tips my food onto the floor.

"Dogs eat down there," she says.

She takes my empty plate and cutlery and sits back at the table.

From here, I can see Megan's legs, crossed at the ankles. In front of me, my gravy sits like a puddle. Peas, sausages and potatoes sink into the floor.

I know I have no choice. I bend my head and start to eat.

• • •

Megan is sitting alone on the front lawn as I go to get my bike. She doesn't look up at me. She's making holes in blades of grass and threading other ones through. There's a long line of green, stretched across her skinny knees. I want to scrunch it up and send it, shredded, into the sky.

My dad's old bike sits against the wall. It's mine now, since I grew out of my pink one. I wheel it out toward the path, feeling it cold and steady under my fingers.

"You're going out again?" Megan says. I don't mean to look at her, but I do. She's stopped threading grass and her hands are resting beside her. "Are you going to Jennifer's?" I wheel my bike past her and answer her with the silence of my back. "Can't you stay and hang out here?"

"It's not my fault you haven't got any friends," I say over my shoulder.

The gate clicks open under the thumb of my free hand. I let it swing closed behind me.

"June?" I hear Megan say, but I won't turn around. I'll let her watch as I ride off, my pedals getting faster in the wind.

At Blister's house, I quietly push open the door to Tom's room.

Blister looks up as soon as I walk in.

"Hey," he says.

"June!" Tom's face lights up. He's lying on his back on the bed and I go over and stroke his hair.

"How are you doing, Tomski?"

"I'm OK," he says.

Blister's cupped hand beats firmly on Tom's chest, over and over. Tom lies patiently, staring at the paper shapes dipping down from his ceiling. They turn slightly in the warm air that drifts in through the window.

Blister doesn't need to ask me to help Tom sit up. Together, we move his little brother until his back is against the wall. He feels so fragile. I'm always surprised that his bones don't snap under the pressure.

"OK. Copy my breathing," Blister says. They breathe slowly and hold the air in. I can hear the crackles in Tom's chest, and when he coughs his whole body shakes. The mucus rattles as his lungs try to get it free.

It never gets easier seeing him like this. I want to scoop him up and run with him to a place where he'll never hurt again.

"OK?" Blister asks as Tom coughs sticky mucus into the bowl I hold. Tom nods and finally flops onto his side. I put the bowl on the floor and sit down next to him on the bed, so I can hold him.

"Your skin's beautiful, June," Tom says as he strokes my arm. His words stop me.

"Do you really think?" I ask.

"I really think," Tom says. And I want to hug him so much that his loveliness soaks into me and never disappears.

"Do you think Mom and Dad will let me get a pig?" Tom asks.

"A pig?"

"I could look after it," Tom says. "And it's not like a dog—it wouldn't need to be taken for long walks."

"I've never heard of a pig as a pet," I say.

"It wouldn't kill birds like a cat does."

"You could always ask them," Blister smiles, paddling his hands gently in the center of Tom's back.

"Can pigs climb stairs?" Tom asks seriously.

"I have no idea," Blister laughs.

"I bet they can," I say.

"It'd sort of run and wobble up," Tom says. "It could sleep in my room."

"It'd stink," Blister says.

"I wouldn't mind. I'll keep my window open."

"In winter?"

"He'd keep me warm."

"A big hot-water bottle."

"A smelly one." And Tom giggles his fragile laugh that always makes me happy and sad at the same time.

"How about a salamander?" Blister asks.

"A lizard?" I ask, screwing up my nose.

"At least they're not smelly," Blister says.

"And I bet they can climb stairs," Tom adds.

"June and I could get you one. It can't be hard." Blister puts a pillow behind Tom's back. "We could bring it back in my bag."

"Could you?" Tom's eyes are wide.

And I know we will. Blister and I will find Tom his salamander. We'll bring it into his bedroom and we'll watch his face shine as it jumps onto his bed and scuttles away across the floor.

. . .

"I think I want to be a doctor," Blister says to me as we pedal away from his house.

"I'd like to be one, too," I say, thinking of Tom, sleeping in his bed when we left.

"I thought you wanted to be a vet." The wind catches Blister's words and brings them to me.

"I'm not sure anymore."

"Imagine, we could be doctors together."

"We could find a cure for Tom's cystic fibrosis," I say as I speed past him and race him to our trailers.

Around the back of our art room, the wall is creeping green where the sun never touches it. It feels scaly under my fingers.

"We should wash it," I say idly, but Blister is already climbing over the fence and jumping down the other side.

We walk along the edges of the trees. They are completely still, stretching their arms wide. There's something about being in this part of the forest that makes me scared, but it's our only way to the stream.

Among the trees it's darker, but the trapped air is warm. The smell of bark sits on me. When I breathe, it moves inside.

"Do you really think we'll find a salamander?" I ask. My voice is quieter than our feet as they crack through the forest floor.

"Maybe." Blister suddenly puts his arm on mine to stop me. "Listen."

There it is. The sound of water slipping among the trees. We walk more quickly, almost running. Blister's bag bumps up and down on his back.

The stream is tiny here. A thin line moving through the wet grass. We bend down to touch it, letting the cold sweep over our hands.

"It's funny how it just keeps on going," I say.

"And the bit of water we see, right now, is gone," Blister says, putting his other hand in it, to make a dam with his knuckles. The water builds up slightly, but then pushes around the side. "We could put all the stones in the world in front of it, but it'd still find its way through."

I imagine Kathleen facing the wall of water. She doesn't have time to scream before she's washed away.

I shake my wet hands in the air. The cold on my skin disappears.

"Shall we walk for a bit?" Blister asks.

"I'm going to walk in the stream," I reply.

"I knew you would," Blister laughs.

"Maybe I'll spot some salamander eggs." I take off my sandals and loop them through my fingers.

"It's cold," I say as the water soaks my ankles.

"Of course it is."

"It's nice, though." I want to stand and watch my feet underneath the rippled glass, but Blister has started walking.

"Did you know that salamanders regenerate their lost limbs?" Blister asks. The stream hisses gently at me.

"So their legs can just grow back again?"

"I think so. And other damaged parts of their body too."

If Tom was a salamander, maybe he could grow new lungs.

"Look." Blister is pointing to thick grass at the bottom of a tree.

"What?"

"There's a snake."

I stop still.

"It's an adder, I think," he says. Slowly, he creeps forward. I watch as the gap between us gets bigger.

"Don't, Blister," I say quietly, putting my sandals on my wet feet.

"It's not moving."

"Then it's sleeping. That's even worse, if you wake it."

Blister leans down carefully toward it.

"I think it's definitely an adder," he whispers.

"It'll hurt you, Blister." I'm edging toward him. I want to pull him back, to where he's safe.

"I've always wanted to see one close."

"You've seen it now."

"I don't think it's asleep," he says. "I think it's hurt."

He kneels down, right next to the snake. It doesn't move. I walk forward slowly, wishing my feet wouldn't make a sound.

"It's been bleeding," Blister says, pointing toward the coil of brown in the grass. There's a big bubble of dried blood cracking out of the snake's skin.

It must sense us. It uncurls slightly and tries to lift its head. I grab Blister back, but he doesn't move.

"I don't think it can hurt us," he says quietly. The snake begins to roll strangely back on itself. "We need to help it." Blister looks up at me.

"How?"

"We'll take it back to our trailers. When I get home, I'll ask my dad what to do."

"To make it better?"

Blister nods. "Maybe Tom would like it more than a salamander."

I look at the snake, shuddering in the grass.

"OK."

Blister slides his hands along the knotted ground. He hesitates slightly, but then pushes them underneath the snake. I know he's a bit scared, even though he's pretending that he isn't.

"Are you just going to pick it up?" I ask.

He nods. "I'll carry it in my bag."

"I think that would scare it."

"I'll just carry it, then," he says.

"Hold your hands around its neck so it can't bite you."

"I don't think they have necks." Blister laughs a bit shakily.

The snake goes still as Blister picks it up.

"It knows we're trying to help it," I say.

We walk in silence. The snake's tongue darts in and out, but I think it's slower than it should be. Part of me wants to put my hand in front of it, to let its tongue touch my skin, just to see.

The forest seems smaller now, as if it's closed in on us slightly. I want to tell it that we will look after its snake. I whisper the words in my head and hope that it can hear.

The snake begins to writhe slightly again.

"Do you think it's hurting?" I ask.

"I don't know. I hope not."

Outside the forest, we walk in the heat across the grass. I steady Blister, as he steps over our fence, his eyes on the split brown skin in front of him.

"I think we should keep him in the school trailer," he says.

"Inside?"

"If we leave him outside, an animal will eat him." Blister itches his nose with his shoulder. "We'll need some grass to make him comfortable."

I rip up handfuls of the long grass beside our path, then follow them up the steps, my arms full of the dry green.

Our snake bucks slightly as Blister lays him down on the nest I've made. Then he's still.

"What if he just slides off it and gets lost in the trailer?" I ask.

"He's too ill, I reckon."

I lie down on my belly so that I'm facing the snake.

"We need to name him," I say.

"OK." Blister sits cross-legged next to me on the floor.

I look into our snake's eyes. Round beads stare back at me, unblinking.

"You're going to be OK," I tell him. His tongue moves out slowly at me in reply. I smile up at Blister. "He's trying to talk to me."

Suddenly, Blister throws himself forward, pushing me away. There's a shooting pain in my wrist. The snake hisses at me and curls back again, rocking on the silent grass.

"Did it get you?" Blister asks, with panic in his eyes.

"Yes." I look up at him, but my wrist is hurting and I don't know what else to say.

He grabs my arm and is pulling me out and down the steps.

"Wait here," he says, but his words haven't got the right breaths. "Don't touch the bite. I'll get my dad." He's already sprinting away.

"No," I shout. "He'll tell my dad and Kathleen. If she finds out about you she'll stop us seeing each other."

Blister runs back to me.

"You have to get to the hospital, June."

"I'll bike home. I'll go from there."

My wrist is going red. Already my skin looks puffy with the poison underneath it.

"It'll take too long."

"I'll risk it," I say. Blister knows I mean it.

"Quickly, then. I'll come with you."

"Not to my house."

He's dragging me again. We're climbing over the gate.

"I'll stay with you until you're almost there." He picks up my bike and holds it steady, as I climb onto it. "Can you do this? You've got to try to keep your arm still."

"Yes." But my hand feels distant on the handlebar.

"Hurry," Blister says, and we pedal our bikes along the track and in among the trees.

"OK?" Blister looks over at me.

"Yes."

But it feels like a bruise is being drawn up my arm.

"Was it definitely an adder?" I ask.

"I think so." He stares straight ahead.

We bike along the road. Blister is fast and I have to keep up with him.

"What if they see you?" I ask.

"It won't matter," he says, as he keeps pedaling ahead.

"It will." *It will, Blister, it will.*

Near my house I stop and he has to stop too.

"I'll go on my own now."

"What if they're not home?" Blister looks like he might cry.

"They will be."

"Go straight there." He looks down at my arm. "Quickly."

So I put my feet back on the pedals and start to move.

"I'll see you soon," I say, but I don't look back.

Around the corner, my house stands looking blankly at me. I get off my bike, unclick the gate and go through.

I leave my bike tipped on the grass. My arm feels heavy now, but I can't tell whether it hurts anymore. My elbow pulses in time with my steps.

I open the front door, but the house is silent.

"Dad?" I call quietly, but no one replies.

The kitchen is empty. In the living room, I see them all through the window. They're clustered together in the backyard—my dad, Kathleen and Megan. It looks so wrong.

I stand and watch them. The pain in my arm heaves up again. I glance down at my swollen skin.

My dad finally looks up and sees me. He smiles and waves, beckoning me to join them. I stare back. It's enough to make him stand up and walk inside.

• • •

The hospital is very white. I've never been in one, apart from when I was born. I didn't come here when my mom died. It was too late.

I am in a wheelchair and they're pushing me along. My dad is running beside me. Kathleen and Megan are somewhere parking the car. I hope they lose their way and don't come in.

It's very bright in here. There are lots of windows on either side of the corridor, but still the long lights are shining on the ceiling.

"How long ago?" the doctor asks my dad.

"About an hour."

The doctor nods. Light brown skin, peeking out of a stark, white coat.

We stop in a room and they lay me on a bed. They give me pills to swallow and they prod my bulbous arm.

"And it was definitely an adder?" The doctor peers at me kindly.

"I think so."

I want to sleep and look at the round eyes of the snake again. Perfect circles, just watching me.

"It was dying," I say. The doctor nods his head again, as he hooks a plastic bag filled with liquid to a pole.

"Where did you find it?"

"By a river."

And Blister picked it up and carried it back.

"Near Creekend Pool," I lie.

There's a heaviness under my skin. A seeping of the snake into me.

"Kathleen will be here soon," my dad says. His fingers touch my other hand.

"Don't let her in."

The doctor attaches a drip to the pole next to the bed. The liquid bulges in the bag.

"You've been one lucky lady," the doctor says to me, his words crinkled around the edges. "Any other snake and things would have been very different."

"But you shouldn't have touched it," my dad says.

"It was dying."

"Snakes can still bite you up to an hour after they've died," the doctor says.

"I didn't know that," my dad says.

The ceiling is painted smooth. If it was water, I'd like to swim in it. It'd cool me down.

I look back to the doctor and he smiles at me. I think he has kindness in his bones. When I'm alone with him, I'll tell him everything. He'll make the bite better and he'll make everything else better too.

The door opens. I don't look, because I already know. I sense the two of them there, before they even say anything.

"June," Kathleen says, and I hear her rushing toward me. Now the doctor won't be able to save me.

"This must be Mom," the doctor says, and he smiles for her, too, as he reaches out and shakes her hand.

AFTER

"I didn't tell anyone what Kathleen was doing," I say. "Not properly."

"Why was it so difficult to tell?" Reverend Shaw asks gently.

"Have you ever been scared?" I ask him.

"Yes."

"But *really* scared. So scared that your thoughts shut down and you can't see, or hear, or think properly?"

"No," Reverend Shaw says. "I've never been that scared."

"I have."

"I know you have." He reaches over and touches my arm gently. "It must have felt impossible to ask for help."

"At the time it did. But now I want to find the little girl I was and tell her not to be afraid. I want to take her hand and help her say the first few words. Just the first few words is all it would take. I wish I'd had the courage then."

"It wasn't about courage. You had that. It was about

opportunity and faith in human nature. Yet your faith in that was being destroyed."

"But there were good people too, who would have listened. They would have helped me if they'd known. They could have saved me," I say. And the pain of it crushes me so hard that I curl my head into my knees.

"Never blame yourself for that, June. You were just a little girl."

I hear Reverend Shaw open his Bible. The pages are thin and sound like water. He pauses and then he takes a deep breath.

"Suffering produces endurance," he reads. "And endurance produces character and character produces hope." I feel his hand gently on my back. "And hope does not put us to shame."

I let his words hold me. They fold around me and I try to let them keep me safe.

BEFORE
fourteen years old

I look at the leaflet in front of me and try again. It says to sweep the powder over the lid and make it darker in the hollow of the eye. But, when I do, it just looks like someone has punched me. I rub at my eyes with a tissue and start over. I thought it'd be easier than this morning, but it's not.

I imagine my mom next to me. If she was here, she'd take the brush and dab it on my eyelids. She'd make it perfect.

I want her to untangle herself from those weeds, swim through the biting water and come back to me. I want her to be my mom again.

Megan comes in as I try to wipe the mascara wand through my eyelashes without making big clumps. In the reflection, I can see her leaning on the doorframe.

"What are you doing?" she asks. She sounds like she genuinely wants to know, but I ignore her.

I stroke the wand through my other eyelashes. I'm scared to blink in case it smudges. If Megan wasn't in here, I could go wrong and start again. She watches in silence as I finish and put the make-up back on the table.

"Is it difficult?" she asks.

"I don't want to talk to you," I say coldly. She looks upset, briefly, and then she's suddenly angry.

"Well, there's no point in you wearing make-up," she says. "You'll never look pretty."

I get up and push her roughly out of the way as I go out. She has to move so I can close the door behind me.

"It's my room," I tell her.

"I wouldn't want to go in there anyway," she says, and she walks away, jerking her head back so that her hair sweeps out. "I wouldn't want to touch all of your dust."

I want to hit her, but I keep walking down the stairs, out of the house. I get on my bike and I'm gone.

I don't go too fast. If I do, it makes my eyes water and that'll make my make-up smudge. And I want to stay looking nice.

I've cycled down this path so many times that I could ride with my eyes closed. I love it. It feels like the road to freedom, with my best friend waiting at the end.

I lean my bike against the gate and climb over. It's a cloudy day, but warm, the sort of day that makes our trailers look a bit worn.

The paper streamers that Blister and I strung from the kitchen to the bones room has been battered by last weekend's storm and it trails down limply.

Blister isn't in the art room. He's in the school room, as I thought he'd be, sitting on a beanbag with a big book open on his lap. I look at him through the window while he doesn't know I'm here.

He's so different from the boy I first met. He's taller than me now and his face has gotten older. His shoulders are broader and he wears big sneakers, rather than the small sandals he used to have. He still has glasses held together with tape, since Si sat on them.

When he reads, it's like the rest of the world disappears. I wish I was like that.

Something makes him sense I'm here. He looks up and smiles.

"What are you doing out there?" he asks.

"I didn't want to disturb you," I say as I go up and through the door.

"That's not like you," he grins, putting a piece of paper into the pages of the book and closing it. "What's on your face?"

I reach up to touch my eyes. "Make-up," I say quietly.

"Why?" he asks. I shrug. And suddenly, for the first time ever, I wish I wasn't here. "You don't look right."

I didn't think Blister would be like this. Cherry and Lauren teased me at school today, but I didn't think Blister would.

"So?" I say. I have a rush of sadness and anger that I don't know what to do with.

Blister is just looking at me strangely, as if he doesn't like me anymore.

I jump down the steps and run down our path.

"June!" Blister shouts after me. But I block him out, scramble over the gate and yank my bike upright. "Where're you going?"

Away. Away from it all. I'm going to bike and bike until I get to the edge of the earth.

I'm crying so loudly that I can't hear anything else. I don't even know that Blister has followed, until I see him biking along beside me.

"Stop!" he shouts. I look forward and keep going. He speeds up and swerves in front of me. My bike crashes into his and I fly from it. There's so much pain in my arm and my hip when I land.

Our bikes lie tangled together on the bumpy ground.

Blister kneels beside me, shaking his head.

"June?" He's here. Beside me.

"I'm OK," I say, sitting up.

"Have you broken anything?" Blister asks.

"I don't think so. I just hurt."

"I'm sorry." He puts his hand awkwardly in mine. "I didn't mean that you don't look nice. It's just that you don't need it." He's going red, but I can't tell whether it's because he's hurting from the fall. "You look pretty enough without it."

"Why do you say that when I'm not?"

"What do you mean, you're not? You must know that you're pretty, June."

"I know I'm not. Ryan and Lauren tell me all the time."

"But I've told you not to believe them. You mustn't believe them. You can't let them win."

I drop my head and the tears are different now. Exhausted, weary tears that never want to stop.

Blister puts his arms around me and we sit, huddled together on the path.

"They make me angry, June," he says quietly. "They're the only thing that really makes me angry."

And I hate the fact that they do. Gentle, lovely Blister, who makes paper shapes and makes me laugh, feels anger because of them.

"Come on," he says suddenly, getting up. "I want to show you something."

I stand up next to him and dust off my shorts. The scrape on my knee is bleeding and I've got blood on my hand.

"Are you OK?" Blister looks concerned.

"It's just a scratch," I say, even though it really hurts.

I wipe underneath my eyes and black mascara comes away on the inside of my thumb.

Blister smiles. "I think you've ruined your make-up." Then he looks all serious again. "You really don't need it, June."

We pick up our bikes. They're a bit scratched, but they work fine. We cycle back to the trailers, side by side. The sun's heat is on my arms; it dries the blood on my knee. My legs hurt a bit as they move around, but I don't care.

"This way," Blister says, leading me down the path toward our fifth trailer. I've only ever been in it once. Blister says it's where the ghosts live. There's a shady patch near it where we like to sit. The best wildflowers grow here.

"Hang on," Blister says, and he puts his hand over my eyes. I let him. I trust him completely. With his other hand, he guides me. "Watch your step." I lift my leg up slightly, but it feels like I'm only stepping over air. "Right," he says, as we stop and I feel his hand move away. "You can open them."

In front of me, the flowers are covered in tons of paper butterflies. It's so beautiful, so brilliant, that I breathe in and cover my mouth.

"I thought you'd like it." Blister beams as I bend down to touch one. Its wings are made from purple tissue paper, covered in dots. "They're for you."

I get up and throw my arms around him. I never want to move from here. Ever. I feel Blister hug me back and he's laughing and happy.

We walk among the butterflies. Each one of them is beautiful.

"They're moving," I whisper.

"It's only the breeze."

"No, they're definitely moving." And I swear they are. I promise I see their wings beat.

Blister and I go into the long grass and sit down, surrounded by butterflies.

"I made most of them at home so you wouldn't see," he says.

"Did you show your mom?"

"No, only Chubbers. He sat with me on the bedroom floor while I made them. Some of them have his jam fingerprints for patterns."

I unhook a blue butterfly from a piece of grass and bring it so close to my eyes that I can see its heartbeat. I'm going to take this one home and keep it safe in my box of precious things.

"Would it die?" I ask.

"Would what die?"

"If you put jam on a real butterfly, would it die?"

"I don't know."

"Its wings would stick together. And if the jam was on its feet, it would weigh it down."

Blister nods, pushing up his glasses on his nose. "Maybe you're right."

"I've heard that if you even touch a butterfly's wing, it'd die."

"Not a paper one though," Blister laughs.

So I touch one. "I love them, Blister. They're the nicest thing anyone's ever done for me." I lean over and kiss him on the cheek.

And, in my mind, I scoop up every one of my butterflies and push them down into my heart. I'll keep them safe and they can beat their wings and no one will ever know that they're there.

· · ·

"I don't think June would do that," Kathleen says. She tries to hold my hand, but I keep my fist clenched and I won't let her. She's sitting as close to me as she can get and I know that if I looked at her I'd see her false worry lines cracked deep into her skin.

"I'm afraid that she did," Mrs. Andrews says. "It was in the middle of the class yesterday. The teacher saw everything."

I feel Kathleen turn to look at me. I stare straight to the front.

"June?" she asks, her voice sweet as sugar. I don't reply.

"June," Mrs. Andrews continues, "this is a very serious offense."

"They made me do it," I say.

"Who?"

"Lauren and Cherry. They were laughing at me." I move my head so I'm looking Mrs. Andrews directly in the eye. She'll see the truth there. She'll come and help me.

"I'm not saying that they were right to do that, June, but you were completely wrong to hit Cherry."

I stare at her. She'll know. She'll know about Kathleen.

"I can't just let this go. I'm going to have to suspend you for three days. You won't be coming back to school until next Monday."

"But I won't be at home to look after her," Kathleen says. "I'll be at work."

"I'm sorry, I've no option, Mrs. Kingston," she says. Kathleen has all her attention. I may as well have vanished in a puff of smoke.

"That's OK. We'll work something out. And she won't do it again," my dutiful stepmother says.

"Maybe a small punishment at home would work too," Mrs. Andrews continues. "Banning their mobile phones seems a good idea these days."

Kathleen nods. "Don't worry, I'll have a long talk with her. She's a good girl. It won't happen again." She stands up and strokes my hair. She doesn't try to take my hand again.

"We'll see you on Monday, June," Mrs. Andrews says. "Mrs. Kingston, I'll be in touch to tell you how June is getting on."

She closes the door behind us. The corridor is empty. All the children have gone home. I walk with Kathleen in silence toward the car. Megan is sitting in the passenger seat. She looks at me as though she wants to ask a question, but she doesn't say a word.

They talk all the way home, as though I'm not here. About their day, about Megan's math class, about Shannon's party.

If I opened the car door and jumped out now, I could roll along the ground and then run away. I'd be so quick into the forest that they wouldn't know which way to turn. I'd go deeper and make my home there, in a little dark cave, with berries to eat.

The car stops. We're at the house. Kathleen and Megan get out first and I follow them inside. Megan scuttles up the stairs to her room.

I wait, with my coat on and my bag over my shoulder.

Kathleen goes into the kitchen.

She doesn't come out.

I put my bag on the floor, take off my coat and hang it on the peg.

Her hand grabs me roughly. She drags me by my hair into the kitchen. Her other hand is over my mouth, so my scream gets stopped in her palm.

She pushes me into a chair, pulls my head back and forces a handful of ice cubes into my mouth and down my throat.

The pain breaks my brain. There's a choking, gurgling noise coming from me and it feels like the freezing cubes have cut me. I'm going to suffocate on my own blood.

And I'll never say goodbye to Blister.

He'll never know.

The room is beginning to fade. It's going black at the edges.

Kathleen tilts me forward and I cough them out. They're just ice cubes. They haven't sliced my throat. I'm not bleeding.

Before she can touch me again, I run from her. I hold my hand to my neck. My skin is still here. I'm still here. I watch my feet run up the stairs. I do exist. They're my shoes, my socks. It's my hand on the door handle. My arm. My hair that I touch. My breathing.

And each one of my breaths shows she hasn't won.

• • •

"June." Mrs. Wick looks up at me from the plant pot by the kitchen window. "Why aren't you at school?"

"Our teacher's sick," I lie.

"So they sent the whole class home?"

"Yes." I don't look her in the eyes, not when she's so kind to me.

"What about the other teachers?"

"I don't know," I say, and shrug. Through the window I can see Si, Chubbs and Mil. They're sitting together on the ground, deep in conversation.

"Lucky us, then," Mrs. Wick smiles, although I don't think she believes me. "Do you want to help me with this?"

"OK." I look over my shoulder for Blister, but he's not here.

The plant pot stretches along the length of the window. It has a thin layer of soil in it. She pats it down, seeming not to notice the crumbling bits sinking under her nails.

"Their dad is teaching them about the energy from plants. They're all scattered around the yard somewhere. Could you hold this?" She passes me a small trowel. "I'm probably too late with these, but I'm going to give it a go."

Mrs. Wick rips open the packet of seeds and sprinkles them thinly on top of the soil.

"Do you want to put the soil over the top?" she asks.

There's a bag of compost leaning against the wall. She holds it open for me so that I can duck the trowel in, scoop it up and sprinkle it over the top of the waiting seeds.

"What are you growing?" I ask, bending down for more compost.

"Supposedly cattleya. But I was meant to plant them a couple of months back. They'll be pretty if they grow, though." She pats the earth flat over the top. "Did your mom like plants?" Her question takes my breath for an instant. I hadn't expected it.

"Yes."

Mrs. Wick goes to the sink and fills a vase with water. She comes back and pours it slowly over the soil.

"Do you have a yard?" she asks.

"A little one. Mom and I used to plant things together."
She'd sing to the flowers to help them grow.

"And now?" She dries her fingers on her apron.

"Now I don't go out there much."

Mrs. Wick looks at me as though she's trying to work something out. As though I'm a puzzle that she can't quite solve.

• • •

I sit on Blister's bed, my back to the wall. His room is tiny. His dad divided his and Maggie's room, so that they could have their own space. If I stretch my legs out straight, they can almost touch the other wall.

Blister sits on the chair next to his bed. It doubles as a table, so he's had to move his books and clock to the floor.

"What's the real reason, then?" He looks at me intently. I know what he's asking and I don't want to lie.

"I got suspended."

"What does that mean?"

"I'm not allowed to go back to school until Monday."

"That doesn't seem to be much of a punishment."

I smile. "We can hang out together."

"Don't you have to stay at home?" Blister asks.

"Dad and Kathleen are at work. They won't know."

"Oh, right."

"And Kathleen confiscated my mobile phone."

"Well, that's no punishment either."

"Because I haven't got any friends to call?" I laugh, even though the words hurt a bit.

"If I had a phone, you could call me," Blister says seriously.

"It wouldn't work from your house anyway."

Blister nods. "What did you do, to get suspended?"

"I hit Cherry," I say.

Blister whistles softly. "What was she doing to you?"

I shrug. "Just being mean."

"But what?" Blister persists. I look him right in the eyes. He's my friend. He'd never say the things they do.

"That my mom deserved to die."

Blister sits so still, but red creeps into his face. I realize that his fingers are clenched so much that his knuckles have gone bright white. I hate making him feel this way.

"It's OK," I say.

"No, June, it's not."

"I know," I say quietly.

"You know it's not true, don't you?" he asks. I don't blink as he looks at me. "Your mom was worth all of them put together."

"She was beautiful, Blister."

"I know she was."

"And she was kind," I say as Blister leans forward with his elbows on his knees. "And she was the best mom."

"Of course she was. She made you."

There's something in the air between us that's never been here before. It's so strong I can almost touch it. I breathe deeply to push it away.

The door flings open and Maggie is standing here, her face fuming.

"Blister, have you been in my room?"

"No," he says, straightening his back against the chair.

"Someone has definitely been in my room."

"It wasn't me."

"Si!" she screams, turning away from us and stomping down the hall.

The air has changed again. It's just our friendship back.

"Blister!" Mr. Wick yells up the stairs. "We're waiting for you."

"I'd better go," I say, but my chest hurts at the thought of biking back home.

"Don't," Blister says. "Come and join our school for the afternoon. Experience lessons Wick style."

He doesn't wait for my answer. He takes my hand and we go down the stairs.

. . .

My bed has been soaked with water. I didn't realize it before I got in and now my pajamas are wet too. I lift the sheet. Underneath it, the mattress is sodden. I strip off the duvet cover, but inside it's already damp. I roll up the cold sheet and throw it on the floor.

The mattress is difficult to lift and turn over, but I get it flat and push it back into place.

This side is soaked too. It'll take days to dry out.

I curl up on the floor and pull the duvet around me. I'm a bird in a nest. I have wings so strong that I'll fly away. Over the treetops, up to the clouds, through the blue, until I'm swallowed by the warm of the sun.

There's a knocking of something on my window. I open my eyes, but I don't know where I am. I'm warm, but my side aches and, even in the almost dark, I know the room isn't how it's meant to be.

Slowly, the pieces come back together and I remember the mattress. I'm on the floor.

The knocking comes again. I'm unsteady as I stand up and

pull my curtains back, just a crack. Blister is down there waving his arms madly. His bike is next to him on the grass. He's beckoning me to go down. I want to, but my mind is blurry. It's the middle of the night, but even if I was curled up in my bed I'd still prefer to be outside with Blister.

I nod at him and disappear from his view. My drawer squeaks slightly as I open it. I hold my breath, though I know that won't make it silent. I pull out a T-shirt, a sweatshirt, some jeans.

When I'm dressed, I open my door. I expect to see Kathleen, just waiting on the other side. Waiting to force me back onto the soaked mattress. But no one is there.

There are no sounds. I creep, so slowly, down the stairs, clutching the banister so that I don't fall. I've never felt my heart beat so clearly. The blood pulses through it and into my brain.

At the bottom, I step into my shoes and get my coat from the hook. I put it on, but I won't zip it up, as I'm scared it'll make too much noise.

The deadbolt on the door grates slightly as I turn it, but the door opens and lets me go.

Blister is standing here, his smile wide in the moonlight. He puts a finger to his lips.

"Where's your bike?" he mouths. I point to the side of the house. He wants me to get it.

The grass is quiet under my feet. My bike is silent for me. I wheel it out and join Blister as he goes down the path.

As soon as we're through the gate at the bottom, we get on and start to pedal and don't look back.

We're the only ones here. There are no cars, no people. The whole world is sleeping, apart from us. I've never been outside in the middle of the night. I want to shout as loud as I can. I stand up, pedaling fast, our bike lights shining lines through the darkness. For the first time in my life, I feel I could do anything.

We're heading to our trailers. I watch Blister's blue coat puffing out slightly as he bikes ahead of me. This is happy. Because they don't know where I am, that I've gone. I could just keep going forever.

Blister slows down to a stop.

"I didn't want to bike through the forest," he says. "I came the long way around."

I look deep into the trees. I love the way that they stand in line, with so many secrets weaving through the dark between them. I want to go in. I want to be smothered in that kind of fear, one I can control, but Blister is scared.

"Let's go on the path, then," I say, and he looks relieved. So we bike on, keeping the trees beside us.

"Why the middle of the night?" I ask.

"I've thought of a way to speak to your mom," he says. I nearly fall from my bike.

"What do you mean?" I'm angry. Just like that. I wanted this to be only us, being happy.

"I've been reading about it. It's called a séance." He keeps glancing at me and then back to our beams of light.

"A séance?"

"Yes, you can talk to the spirits."

"I know what it is."

We ride on in silence again, looping around the edge of the forest. The magic has gone, though. That excitement that filled my whole body has fizzled up and vanished and drops of anger are in its place.

We get to the gate. The wood of it feels damp. Blister clicks on a flashlight and shines it briefly at my face, then slightly to the side.

"You don't think it's a good idea?" He sounds genuinely disappointed. "I've read a lot about it. I think it could work."

I feel guilty now. Blister has done all this for me. It's deep in the night and he's out in the cold and dark to try to help me. And I know I'd do anything to see my mom again.

"We could find out that she's happy," he says. His face is very vague in the dark, but I can imagine his expression.

"OK," I say.

Our trailers look so different, nestled silently in the dark grass. It's as if they're sleeping. They shine bright white when the beam from the flashlight hits them, and I think they want us to leave them to rest. Our paper streamers are hanging between them again and splashing faded color.

"Come on," Blister says, and he takes my hand. He's going to the fifth trailer, the one we never use. I pull him back slightly.

"It's OK," he says. "I've been in there on my own. It's not so bad."

The door sounds as if it hasn't been opened in years. Inside, the smell of damp soaks into me. I swallow to try to get rid of it, but it just goes deeper.

Blister swings the flashlight around inside. The walls show where the tables and seats were once attached. The floor is warped and covered in grime. In the middle, there are things that Blister must have prepared.

"I read all about it," he says, pulling me toward the black cloth in the center. "You OK?"

"I don't know." My voice sounds strange in this splintered

dark. "I've heard this could be dangerous. That sometimes you call up spirits that won't let you go."

Blister sticks the flashlight into a mug so that it shines toward the ceiling.

"That won't happen if I burn some sage first." His voice shakes slightly.

"But what if the bad ones still come through?"

I stare at him. I want us to get out of here. But he's done all this for me, because he wants me to find my mom. And I know that I want to find her too. My chest burns with the need to see her, to know she's happy.

"Your mom is a good spirit. She'll make sure the others won't hurt us."

Blister picks up a packet of matches and there's a fizz as he lights one. He picks up some dried green stems and holds the match to it.

The flame catches on a leaf, but it disappears quickly. Blister lights another match and holds it for longer. The leaf fries up before the big, yellow flame shrinks to nothing. Yet it's enough. A thick line of smoke flows steadily to the ceiling. The burning green smell settles on my tongue.

"I'm supposed to say something," Blister says, letting the ash drop to the floor.

"Like what?"

"About the spirits."

"Say it, then."

"Promise you won't laugh?"

"I promise."

Blister coughs slightly. "We welcome only good spirits," he says, all serious, and I try to stop myself but I'm nervous and the laugh just pops out of my mouth.

"You said you wouldn't," he says, looking embarrassed.

"I'm sorry." I'm trying to stop. I take a deep breath and wipe my eyes. "OK. I'm OK now. You can start again."

Blister raises an eyebrow at me, one dimple sinking in slightly.

"We welcome only good spirits. Bad spirits, be banished."

I can't hold it in. The laugh splutters out of me.

"June!" But Blister is laughing too. So much that he topples to the side. My stomach is creased with pain, but I love it. I can't breathe and I never want it to stop.

In the upward flashlight, Blister and I laugh with our arms tight across our stomachs, waiting for the wave to pass. When it does, sadness comes in out of nowhere and sits heavy on my skin.

"Do you think she'll come?" I ask quietly.

"I don't know." Blister looks like he wants it to happen. "I don't think you'll hear her voice, not like you remember it."

"I don't remember it," I say, and Blister shakes his head sadly.

"She might show us a sign, though, that she's here with you."

I nod, not taking my eyes from him. I believe he can do this for me.

"We have to put this under here." He picks up a coin from the middle of the cloth in the middle of the floor and puts it under an upturned glass. "It's from the year she was born." He pushes up his glasses on his nose. "I worked it out."

"That's good."

"Hang on." He takes the coin out from under the glass. "You have to kiss it first."

I feel the tips of his fingers as he passes the coin to me.

I hold it to my lips and close my eyes. It's cold, as my mom's skin must have been.

Blister places it back under the glass.

"Ready?" he asks.

"Yes."

"We both have to put our index fingers on the glass." I do as he tells me. This time, I don't giggle. I don't want to. I don't want anything to stop my mom from coming to me.

"We call on Loretta. Make yourself known to us."

I stare at Blister's face, shining in the dark.

"Shall I say it with you?" I whisper, and he nods.

We repeat the words, over and over, our voices creeping to the corners of the trailer, getting caught under the ruined floor.

We stare at the glass. Nothing is happening.

Please come, Mom.

Our words mix with the sage ash and rattle up against the windows.

Please come, Mom. I need you. I need you to tell me how to escape.

The coin clinks against the side of the glass.

Blister and I stop chanting and stare at each other. We don't move.

"Did you do that?" I ask him.

"I don't think so," he says.

"Mom?" I whisper. I close my eyes.

And I'm sure I hear her. She says my name. It's her voice. I feel her hand on my cheek.

"I'm proud of you, June."

The trailer smells of her, the sweet smell of her perfume.

"Mom," I say, but I can't say anymore.

"I'm sorry I left you."

Her smell begins to fade.

"I love you, June."

And she's gone.

Blister is looking at me.

"What happened?" he asks.

"I think she was here."

"Seriously?"

"Yes." I smile. He looks so proud.

"What did she say?"

"That she loves me."

"Of course she does." Blister leans over and hugs me tight. It's him that's everywhere now. "She always will."

The darkness suddenly creeps back. Maybe this is the trailer where the man strangled his wife. And we're here, alone, and no one knows where we are.

"I'm scared," I whisper.

"Me too. Do you want to go?"

"Yes."

The mug tips over when Blister picks the flashlight from it. It falls softly, but it's enough to make us grab each other's arms and run.

We're out of breath when we get to our bikes. I don't like the sound of us here in the night air. Anyone could hear us. Anyone could get us.

"I'll bike back with you," Blister says, pressing his bike-light on.

"But then you'll have to go back on your own." It's too dark and he's scared.

"I'll be OK. I biked to get you."

"But it's different now."

It is. The darkness has an edge to it.

"Let's go," Blister says, and I follow him and his shaky line of light.

Back on the road, we bike faster. It's freezing on my face. I look straight ahead, following Blister's back. I don't want to know what's on either side of me in the thick air.

I can hear Blister's breath. He wants to get home too.

We don't talk until we're near my house and I see him in the distance, in the doorway. My dad. He's got his coat on. Blister and I stop.

"Turn your light off," I whisper. We watch as my dad goes back inside and then comes out again.

"He's looking for you."

"Yes."

"Shall I come with you?"

"No." I say it too quickly. "I think it'll make it worse."

"OK."

"I think you should go now." If my dad bans me from seeing Blister, I'll die.

"Only if you promise that you'll go straight in. You won't go anywhere else."

"I promise."

"All right."

"Thank you, Blister." He knows what I mean. For everything.

He turns his bike around so silently and there's just the sound of his pedals going around. I watch as the black creeps up on him and brushes him away.

I bike forward and into the light from the house. My dad sees me and runs out.

"June!" He doesn't sound angry. He holds me too tight. "Where were you?"

"I went for a ride," I tell him. He takes my bike and I wait for him as he puts it back against the side of the house.

I follow him and watch him go into the kitchen.

"She's here," he says into the room.

"Thank God." It's Kathleen. She comes out and her skin looks even whiter and her eyes are rubbed red. "Oh, June," she says, and she tries to hug me, but I leave my arms hanging by my side. "I was so worried." She's trying to cry.

My dad closes the front door and leads us all into the living room. They're being quiet. Megan must still be asleep. And they wouldn't want to wake precious Megan.

"Where did you go?" Kathleen asks, her hand on my arm. I move myself away and she looks hurt.

"Kath went to check on you, but you weren't there," Dad says. "She said that you wet your bed, June." He looks awkward. "Is that why you ran away?"

"I didn't run away. I went for a ride."

"In the middle of the night?" Kathleen sounds pained.

"Yes."

"You should have woken me," my dad says. "We could have changed the sheets."

I turn to him and speak slowly enough for him to understand. Slowly enough for him to hear the words I can't say.

"I didn't wet the bed."

"June, I saw the sheet," my dad says. "I felt the mattress."

"It might be a bladder infection," Kathleen says. "We could take you to the doctor?"

"I didn't wet the bed."

"I bet it happens to a lot of teenage girls." My dad glances at Kathleen for reassurance.

"Someone poured water on my bed," I say in one breath, before my mind can catch up.

"June, you don't have to be ashamed," my dad says.

"They poured water all over my bed."

Kathleen looks genuinely shocked. Even I almost believe her.

"Who would do that?" she asks, looking at my dad.

"You," I say. "Megan."

"June, you're being ridiculous now," my dad says.

"They did," I tell him. *And so much more, Dad. Can't you see? Believe me on this and I'll tell you everything.*

"Why would they do that?"

"Because they hate me."

"Don't be stupid," my dad says as Kathleen shakes her head sadly, her eyes wide and innocent and loving.

"It's true." Inside, I'm terrified. My paper butterflies are filling me up, beating hard against each other.

"I've had enough of this, June."

My dad is angry, but he's angry with me.

Please, Dad.

"They've done nothing but love you, June. And, quite frankly, I'm surprised that they keep trying."

I feel the butterflies' wings burning. The pain is overwhelming. I've told him, just the beginning, but he doesn't want to hear.

"Of course we keep trying, Bradley," I hear Kathleen say. "We love her. We'll never give up."

"Well, it's the middle of the night and I've got work tomorrow," my dad says. "June, I'm too tired and angry to be with you right now."

"I'll help make your bed," Kathleen tells me gently. "I can put down a blanket over the mattress, with a fresh sheet on top. It'll be fine."

Dad leans over and gives her a kiss. I have to get away from them.

"I'll do it myself," I say before I push past them and run up the stairs. I'm as loud as I can be. I want Megan woken up. I slam my door hard, grab my duvet and curl up against the wall.

Inside me, paper wings are still burning.

AFTER

"I felt so angry inside," I tell Mickey. "It was just building up and up." We've sat to rest on a wall. Light rain falls on us, but I like the feel of it on my skin. I want it to wash the bad feelings away. "And at school I tried to tell the teachers what the other kids were doing, but they wouldn't listen. All they saw was me getting angry and they punished me for that."

"Life's unfair at times," Mickey says, her words scraping the air. "But you mustn't let the bad weigh your life down. Try to fill the other side of the scales with good things."

"Sometimes it's hard," I say.

"It's important, June. Are you listening to me properly?" Mickey asks earnestly.

"Yes," I tell her.

"Your life is precious. Every day that you're on earth is precious. You have a place. You're wanted."

I want to believe her. I need to take her words and stick them all over my skin and keep them safe there, so I never forget.

"And if you face every day with hope, then you've already won," Mickey says.

Hope. Like a bird, it flies too high above me.

"What if I don't know what to hope for anymore?" I ask quietly.

Mickey takes my hand in hers. "Perhaps hope on its own is enough."

BEFORE
fifteen years old

Blister and I lie on our backs, our feet tucked into the same bucket of water. I can feel his ankles against mine.

"What's that round, bumpy bone on my foot?" I ask. "The one that's pressing into yours?"

"This one?" He lifts out his foot and drops of water spill all over us.

"Yes."

"It's the medial malleolus."

"You know too much for a fifteen-year-old," I say. I watch the edge of a cloud creeping toward the sun.

"You asked," he laughs.

"You shouldn't have known."

I feel him move beside me and suddenly water splashes down all over my face.

I hardly have time to sit up before Blister is cupping more water and chucking it at me.

"You shouldn't have done that," I say dramatically. "Not

when I'm such a great aim." I duck my hand into the cold and splash at him, but miss completely.

Blister laughs, dancing around in front of me.

"Not so good."

So I pick up the bucket. It's heavy and the water sloshes.

"No!" Blister says, backing away.

"Yes," I say, stumbling after him. I lift it onto my shoulder and chase him through the grass. He's not running fast and I throw the water at him and it tumbles down his back. He stops and turns to me, his arms straight out to the side, like a scarecrow.

"You were saying?" I taunt him. His hair is wet too.

"I was saying what a brilliant aim you are."

Blister takes off his T-shirt and wrings it out. Water drips onto the grass. He's squeezing the material in his hands, so he doesn't see me staring at him, at his broad shoulders and his muscles that run in lines down his arms.

He looks up. "What?" he asks, his head on one side.

"Nothing." I look away.

"Your top is wet too."

"I won't be taking mine off."

The air around us suddenly turns sharp.

"How long are we going to stand like this?" Blister asks.

"I don't know."

He's looking at me, as though he knows something is different too.

I walk away toward our kitchen.

When I'm inside, it's a little bit cooler. The elm tree overhangs it and keeps the sun off its roof. It's the only trailer that's not an oven at this time of day.

Blister comes to help me cut open the oranges. I push them

onto the squeezer and twist out the juice. We make enough for a small glass to share.

We sit on the step, side by side, our legs touching. That feeling is still there, so strange that it sort of numbs my brain.

"What did you do, then?" Blister asks. "To get suspended this time?"

"I threw a table at Ryan."

"You picked up a table?"

"I wanted to. But it was more like I tipped it up and shoved it. Someone called Sam kind of got caught in the crossfire."

"Did he get hurt?" Blister asks. I can't tell what he's thinking. Whether he's angry with me, or sad.

"A bit."

"June." He sounds so disappointed.

"I didn't mean to." And it's honestly the bit I feel bad about. I didn't want to hurt Sam. "I think I might've broken his toes."

Blister goes very quiet. I wish he'd shout at me, tell me I've let him down. This silence hurts more. I'm scared he's going to get up and walk away.

I stare at the tiny paper table hanging from our art-room doorway. From here, I can barely see the paper plates and cups we stuck on last summer. We kept dropping them and having to search for them in the long grass.

"You need to talk to someone, June. You've got to tell a teacher how bad things have gotten with Ryan and the others."

"I've told you, I've tried."

"You have to try harder. And tell them how Kathleen treats you at home."

"They'll never believe me."

"They will. If you tell them the truth."

Oh, Blister, I haven't even been able to tell you the whole truth.

"OK. I'll try," I say, just to move the conversation away from here. Blister nods his head and looks back at his hands, clasped together on his knees. He moves his thumbs, one on top of the other, over and over. "What shall we do today?" I ask. Blister shrugs, still staring at his hands. "Let's bike somewhere we've never been."

"That's loads of places," Blister says, and he stretches his legs out as far as he can.

"Left or right?" I ask.

What do you mean?"

"Just pick one—left or right."

Blister nudges up his glasses on his nose. "Left."

"OK, let's get on our bikes and go left," I say. Blister grins at me.

"OK."

He stands and puts his hand out to pull me up, then picks up his damp T-shirt and pulls it on. It sticks to his skin.

"I'll get some water," I say. He waits as I go back inside and put a bottle of water in my bag. I grab a packet of cookies too, although I know I shouldn't.

We get on our bikes outside the gate and turn left, down the bumpy path. The sun is already too hot. It sits in my hair.

At the crossroad, we stop. Blister picks up a small stone. He puts his hands behind his back and pulls them out, fists clenched.

"If you get the stone, we go left again," he says.

I touch the knuckles of his right hand. He uncurls his fingers and his palm is empty.

He smiles. "We go right."

There's no breeze at all. Warm touches the back of my throat as I breathe. Our wheels turning is the only sound we make.

When we get to another crossroad, I pick up a stone and without Blister looking I hide it in my palm.

"Left," I say when he touches the knuckles of my hand.

We head down the straight road. It disappears into the distance, folding into the horizon. There are just fields and fields on either side. Patches of green and dried yellow, spotted with flowers.

"Race you!" Blister suddenly shouts.

"It's too hot," I say. But he's off and to keep up with him I have to pedal fast. My legs ache, but I keep going. I can't catch him, but I try.

It feels like ages before we stop to drink water.

"Let's head for there." Blister points to something in a field, further down the road. It looks like a small building. Maybe it holds some old farm equipment.

"Then we stop?" I'm still out of breath. I need some shade.

"Then we stop."

We bike together in silence. Our wheels crunch slightly on the road beneath us.

It's a wooden shelter, with three walls and a sloping roof. It'd fit maybe ten people, lying side by side. Big planks are missing from the walls, and the roof has come loose at one edge and hangs down slightly. It looks like there was some sort of floor once, but the grass has grown through.

We put our bikes on the ground beside it and go in. It's like being covered in cool water.

"That's better," I say as Blister goes to push at the walls.

"I reckon it's OK," he says.

I take off my bag and pass him the water. I watch him tip his head back, swallow some and wipe his lips with the back of his hand.

"Thanks."

As I drink, he disappears around the back of the shelter. I put the bottle on the floor and follow him.

It's the remains of an old car. Most of it has been burned away and it sits, like a giant skeleton, sticking up from the grass.

Bits of the seats are still stuck inside, like melted old skin.

"Hey, Bonnie," Blister says in a thick drawl. "Someone here's gone 'n' burnt out our car." He blows the tip of his invisible gun and puts it in his pocket.

"Who'd do such a thing, Clyde?"

"Someone's after us." And he grabs my hand and pulls me down low, behind the back of our burned-out car. "Shh, they're coming."

We get our guns out of our pockets. Slowly, Clyde crawls around the edge of the hood, but darts quickly back again.

"There's five o' them."

"Five?"

Clyde nods his head seriously and scratches his cheek as he thinks hard.

"I'll get us out of here, Bonnie. Just follow me."

We skulk around the car again. He looks at me and counts down with his fingers. Three. Two. One.

We're running for our shelter, shooting for our lives. I get one of the men, straight between the eyes. Clyde kills two. We dive through the air and roll to safety.

"They're getting away!" Clyde shouts. The other two have gotten into a car. I jump into the road, lift my gun and aim it at them. I don't want to kill them, so instead I blow both their tires out and they swerve all over the place.

I put my hand on Clyde's arm and push his gun down. We watch as the car hobbles off into the distance.

"They won't bother us no more," Clyde says, and he throws his arms around me. "We did it!"

I stay holding him. I can feel his heart beating into mine. It feels like we share the same one.

My breath is on Blister's neck.

He moves his head back and I feel his lips on mine.

I'm kissing Blister.

Blister is kissing me.

Suddenly, it all makes sense. Nothing else matters. Blister wants to kiss me. And I'm wanting to kiss him back.

His lips taste of the warm air. His arms are tight around me.

My Blister is kissing me.

He pulls away and looks at me.

"Oh," he says quietly. He touches my cheek gently with his fingers. "Did you mind?"

"No."

He kisses my forehead and pulls me tight to him. My head rests under his chin and I breathe him in. The sun is hot on us. His skin is against mine. There's no room in me for anything other than happy.

He holds my hand, as we go back to our rusting car and lean against it, finishing the rest of our water. Blister keeps looking at me as though I'm different.

"What?" I ask. It sounds strange in this space, as though the word should echo back from the glass sky.

"Nothing," he smiles.

I pass him two cookies before I twist the packet around and put them back in my bag. I watch his lips as he crunches them. He wipes the crumbs away with his finger.

"What?" he asks.

"Nothing," I laugh.

But it's everything. And I know now that if the world stopped spinning, Blister and I would survive it all.

We glance at each other again, before we go and pick up our bikes and begin to pedal down the long, dry line stretching in front of us.

. . .

I don't know where I am at first and I lash out with my arms. The light is so bright that it feels like ice.

I'm in my bed. I was asleep. It must be night. The white light sears into me, but I can't close my eyes. Someone is holding them open. Someone else is sitting on my arms, shining a flashlight deep into me. One eye, then the other.

I try to scream, but a hand goes tight over my mouth.

The pain is like nothing I've ever known. I can't blink. I can't close the brightness away. My body knows that every part of this is wrong.

I'm going to be sick, but the hand is a wall, bricking up my mouth. My eyes burn. I writhe around, trying to twist my head and yank myself free from the fingers that grip my eyelids open.

Just when I think I can't bear any more, the flashlight clicks off. I can't see them as they shift out of my room. The memory of the light is still in my eyes. I press my hands over them, but deep, red flashes are piercing there.

My whole body is shaking. I can't stop it. I turn onto my side as a headache begins to slice, layer by layer, through my skin and into my skull.

. . .

"We're having a family day," my dad says firmly the next morning. "I'm not going to discuss it anymore."

"But I don't want to," I say again.

"Well, it's not all about you, June. There are other people in this family too."

"Bradley," Kathleen says gently. She gives him one of her looks that tells him not to be so harsh on me. "It'll be fun," she tells me.

"Please come," Megan says as she holds her toast in front of her mouth. If I didn't know better, I'd think that she genuinely wanted me to be there.

"She is coming," my dad says. "She has no choice."

And I know I don't. If I don't go, he'll ground me and then I won't see Blister.

The heat in the car is unbearable. All four of us roll down our windows as far as we can.

"Where are we going?" Megan asks. Her skinny legs are tucked into the back of the car, next to mine.

"Lazy Creek," my dad says, starting the engine. I look at the back of his head. Has he forgotten that it was Mom's favorite spot? Where we used to go together. "June loves it there." He catches my eye in the rearview mirror and smiles.

I did love it there, when it was us three. My dad, my mom and me. Not like this. I don't want Kathleen there. I don't want her treading her dirt all over our memories.

"You'll love it too, Megan," my dad tells her.

"I can't wait," she says. She turns to look at me. "Will you show me around?" I can tell that she's excited. I just shrug my shoulders and stare out my window.

Blister will be waiting. He'll be sitting on the steps of our trailer, his legs stretched out in the grass, and I won't turn up and he'll think it's because he kissed me.

I clench my teeth shut, to stop myself from screaming.

My dad starts singing at the top of his voice. He's tapping the steering wheel and Kathleen joins in, her voice soft and innocent, wrapping around his words like honey. He reaches out and pats her knee and, as she pulls her blonde hair over her shoulder, I close my eyes tight.

I'll be free I'll be free I'll be free, I say in my head, just like Blister told me to. *I'll be free I'll be free.*

Breathe, June, he says. *Such a deep breath that it takes ten seconds to get it all in and ten seconds to let it out.*

Free free free free.

The car eventually stops and I open my eyes. I remember this clearing as though I came here yesterday: the place to park surrounded by a circle of stones, paths tiptoeing off among the trees. My mom holding my hand and us running off ahead of Dad.

"Shall I carry this?" Megan asks, holding up the blanket.

"That'd be great," my dad replies. "June, can you grab this?" He passes me the green, zipped bag, before he picks up the basket and slams the trunk. "Do you want to lead the way?"

I shake my head and look at him. I don't want to be here, but he doesn't notice at all.

"Follow me, then." His smile is real. He doesn't even try to see me.

I stay at the back, close, but behind them all. Megan wants to walk by my side, but I won't let her. I want to trip her up and watch her tumble to the ground and clog her bleeding knees with dust.

It's not far to the spot where I've been so many times before. A few rocks jut out across the creek, their tops worn flat. They're big enough for all of us to sit on.

"Shall I lay this on the grass?" Megan asks my dad.

"Sounds good," he replies, putting the basket down. Megan throws the blanket wide and stretches it at my feet. I don't help her.

Instead, I go over to the rocks nearest the water and stand at the edge. It's like rippled glass. I bend down and touch the stones underneath it. When I break its surface, it doesn't stop. It just changes direction and works around my fingers.

I love the sound of it. The gentle rushing calms me.

"It's a beautiful spot." Kathleen has come up behind me and she puts her arm around my shoulder. She leans her head into me. I stay completely still. I can't pull away, but having her so close is almost unbearable.

I look at the water and concentrate on its movement. On and on. I try to count to ten, but my mind freezes.

Kathleen kisses the top of my head and as she stands up I can breathe again.

Megan says something to her, but it's as though they're behind a wall, their voices muffling through bricks, far enough away that they can't hurt me.

"Do you want to swim?" My dad is standing next to me. I get up and shake my head. "Was it OK to come here?" he asks quietly. He knows our memories. He must see Mom too.

I shrug, because my answer isn't the one he wants to hear. He faces me, but I stay staring at the creek.

"She'd be so happy that you have another mom who loves you, just as much as she did."

Each and every one of his words picks hard at my chest. I want to scream.

I watch the water. I count to ten.

I bury the hurt.

"Can we eat, Dad?" Megan calls. He turns from me.

"That's a good idea," he says as he walks away, his footsteps soft on the rocks.

. . .

I'm scared to see Blister again. What if I kissed him wrong and he doesn't want to do it again?

What if he waited all day for me yesterday and I didn't come and it was long enough for him to think and decide that it shouldn't have happened and now we've spoiled everything?

My heart thuds in time with the pedals.

What if he's gone and he doesn't ever want to come back?

It's quiet at our trailers. I wait, standing with my bike, hoping for any sound. But there's no sign of Blister.

The air is the hot before a storm.

Quietly, I climb over the gate and walk down the path. The kitchen is empty and he's not in the art room.

I open the door to the school trailer and he's here. He's cutting a shape from a piece of paper and has all the bits of the body dotted around him on the floor.

"It's amazing how we all work, isn't it?" he says, as though I've been here all along. He tilts the paper brain he's holding to show me. I don't really like the way he's cutting up a big, old book, but I won't tell him that. He's bursting with excitement and seems so young again, just like when I first met him. "How all these bits are inside us and we need them all to work properly, for us to live. How the tiniest little thing can make it all go wrong."

"It's clever how it all fits," I say, sitting down among the bits of paper. There's so much of it surrounding us—lungs and a liver and veins and a heart.

"See this?" Blister points with the tips of his scissors to the middle of the paper brain. "Just this little bit is the Broca's area. It helps us understand language, and without it we can't speak."

"If it gets damaged, can it ever be fixed?"

Blister curves the scissors around the edges. "I don't think so. Maybe I'll discover that too."

"At the same time as your cure for cystic fibrosis?"

"And diabetes."

"Dr. Blister."

"I'll have to be Dr. Jacob. Or Dr. Wick."

"Dr. Wick sounds good. Like you're a bit scary and old-fashioned and might use candles to burn bad bits out of people's skin."

"And use those long, burning scissor things," Blister says, adding the brain to the other cut-outs on the floor.

"And leeches."

"That suck your blood." Blister leans in really close to me. He grabs my arm and sucks so hard on it that he leaves a big, red mark.

Then he's kissing me. He's kissing me again.

This time I can breathe, this time I can feel it all. Blister's lips are on mine.

And it's the best feeling in the whole wide world.

We don't stop kissing, and inside me my paper heart beats so hard, the sound of it filling me and filling Blister and our trailer and the whole of our place.

When we stop, Blister looks at me.

"You don't mind?" he asks.

I shake my head and smile and he smiles back and kisses me

for the longest time, until he stops again. He looks so earnest that I almost want to laugh.

"I'm going to stop Kathleen being nasty to you, June. I don't know how I'm going to do it, but I will. I promise you."

He's brought her in here and I want her gone. I lean forward and kiss him again.

But Kathleen is standing here now, hand in hand with Megan.

So I kiss Blister and kiss him again and again, until I make them fade away and disappear.

• • •

The envelope is stuck to my locker. It's got my name on it. It's definitely for me. I take it down, put it in my bag and go to class.

I don't really want to think about it. I don't know what's in it. But my name is in nice writing and it's clean.

I stay sitting in my place, tucked at the back of the classroom, and concentrate on Mr. Lovell's description of tectonic plates. People are laughing and shouting out, but I stay quiet. It's safer like this. I always keep an invisible wall around me now, so that they can't hurt me. They still try, but it's hard for them to get in.

At lunch, it's raining, so I sit with Jennifer and Helen inside. We're at the edge of the lunchroom, the noise spreading out around us.

"I got this," I say, putting the envelope on the table.

"Who's it from?" Helen asks.

"I don't know."

"Haven't you opened it?"

"I have now," I say, ripping the back off it, pretending that I'm calm, that I don't care what's inside.

It's an invitation. To Cassandra's sixteenth birthday party. I check the name at the top. *June*. In clear handwriting.

"Whoa," is the only thing Helen says.

"Lucky you," Jennifer says quietly. "She's nice."

"Didn't you get one?" I ask. Jennifer shakes her head. "You might."

"I doubt it."

"I won't go," I say.

"You should. It'll be good," Jennifer says.

I raise my eyebrows at her. "They'll all be there," I remind her.

"Maybe they've finally grown up?"

"And had complete character transformations?" Helen says.

"Maybe," Jennifer says. "People change."

I turn the invitation over in my hands. The back is completely blank. But the front is beautiful, edged in gold, with flower prints bordering it. There's Cassandra's name, written in swirly writing. And my name at the top.

"I'm pleased for you, June." Jennifer squeezes my arm.

"Next time, you'll come too," I tell her.

She shrugs. "It's OK." But it's not, so I tuck the invitation back into its envelope and put it in my bag. I won't take it out again until I get home.

. . .

"Will you come with me?"

"I don't think you should go," Blister says. We're sitting on our steps, aiming stones at the triangle of old cans we've set up.

"Why?" I've had a strange feeling in my stomach since I got the invitation. I can't tell whether it's excitement, or whether I'm scared.

"You don't think it's a bit weird? That they're suddenly inviting you to a party?"

"It's not them. It's Cassandra. She's not really part of that group. She's just always kind of ignored me."

"That makes her OK, then?" Blister pulls his arm back and throws a stone hard. He knocks the top can clean off.

"So you won't come with me?"

"I didn't say that. I just said I don't think you should go."

"Jennifer says we should always give people a chance to change."

"People like Ryan are never going to change."

"It's not Ryan's party." I've never felt really angry with Blister, but it's scratching at me now. I want him to be happy for me. I want him to say that maybe things will start to change. Things will get better.

The stone I throw is big, but it misses the cans completely.

"I'll come," Blister says. "If you're going to go, I'll come with you."

"Really?"

"Of course. I'm not going to let you go there on your own."

I lean over and kiss him on the lips, but he seems sad and doesn't kiss me back.

"It'll be good, I promise," I tell him, and lean my head on his shoulder.

I see the invitation in my mind, my name at the top. I'll turn up at Cassandra's house with Blister and everything will change. I'll look pretty and I'll be there with a boyfriend and everyone will step back and let us walk through and then they'll all want to talk to us. They'll all want to be our friends.

With one stone, Blister sends the rest of the cans clattering to the ground.

. . .

"You look beautiful," Kathleen says. I stay sitting in the chair, my dad in the armchair opposite. He puts his newspaper down and looks up at me.

He smiles. "You really do."

Kathleen has spent the last half hour straightening my hair. I've hated every second of it.

"Do you want to see?" she asks. She puts down the straightening irons and comes around the front to look at me.

"You look really pretty, June," Megan says. She's been patiently watching, her face clear and innocent, but I know what she's really thinking.

Kathleen takes the mirror from the mantelpiece and holds it in front of me.

I look strange. My curls have gone. I have this long, straight black hair. I want to hate it, because Kathleen has done it.

"Thank you," I say flatly, and get up. "I'd better go, or I'll be late."

"Are you sure I can't drive you?" my dad asks.

"Jennifer's dad is happy to," I lie to him.

"I can take you to their house at least." My dad folds the paper and puts it on the arm of the chair.

"I'd like to bike," I say. I go over and give him a kiss to stop him from getting up.

"OK. If you're sure."

"I am."

"Take your phone and call me if you have trouble getting back."

"I will."

"And have a great time," he says. He looks proud and

concerned all rolled into one.

"Have a lovely time, honey," Kathleen says. She comes toward me and I smell her perfume as she wraps her arms around me. She pulls away and kisses me on the forehead.

I can tell that Megan wants me to say goodbye to her, but I don't. Instead, I walk away and leave my perfect family watching, as I close the door behind me.

• • •

I have to stop the bicycle to pull my skirt tight underneath me. The wind is catching it and I don't want to show my underwear to the world. I keep touching my hair. It feels so different. I can run my fingers through it and they come straight out the other side.

I'm suddenly scared that they won't like it. That if Cherry and Lauren are there, they'll laugh. I've spent so long imagining all the good things that will happen when I walk into the party with Blister that I haven't left room for any bad things. But now they're trickling in. I pedal faster, because I don't want them here.

The Wicks' lane is littered with their things. Chubbers' plastic push toy is half sticking out of a bush. There's a bicycle wheel perched at the edge of the lane and a pair of shorts sitting in the path to their front door.

I leave my bike just inside their gate.

I'm nervous. I'm scared of Blister seeing me like this. But I'm so excited too. We're going out together, me and him. They'll all wonder where I've been hiding my boyfriend.

I smooth down my hair as I walk up the path. Tom opens the door before I even get to it.

"June's here!" he shouts. He doesn't even comment on my hair—he just runs off into the kitchen.

Blister walks down the stairs. I know he notices, as soon as he sees me.

"Hey," he says. He's wearing a blue T-shirt I haven't seen before. And his jeans look washed and ironed. He looks great.

He comes to me and kisses me quickly on the lips and we stand just smiling at each other.

"You straightened your hair," he eventually says.

"Yeah." I shrug, as though it's no big deal, but I can't help touching it.

"It looks nice," he says, but I can tell he's not sure.

"Thanks." Suddenly I want my curls back.

"Dad!" Blister calls. "We're ready to go."

"Coming," his dad replies from somewhere in the house. Blister picks the keys off the hook near the door.

"June," Mr. Wick says, as he comes rushing in. "You look beautiful."

"Thank you."

"Look at you two," he says, standing back.

"Come on, Dad," Blister says. I don't often see him looking embarrassed and it makes me want to hug him.

The three of us go down the steps and Blister takes my hand as we go out toward the car. I squeeze his fingers and he squeezes mine back. And there's happiness in my bones. And even if the party isn't great, if people aren't kind, I know that this happiness is a part of me now and no one can take it away.

Blister and I sit together in the back seat and he reaches over to hold my hand again. I look out the window at the fields disappearing past, but all I can think about is Blister's skin touching mine.

"Still OK for me to pick you up at midnight?" Mr. Wick asks.

"That'd be great," Blister says.

"And that's definitely all right with your dad?" Mr. Wick catches my eye in the rearview mirror.

"He's fine with that," I reply. I take my hair and pull it over one shoulder. It lies flat against my top. If I look down, I can just see the tips of it. It looks a bit like the ends of frayed material.

Blister squeezes my hand and I glance up at him. He smiles and nods at me.

"You'll be fine," he says. "We both will."

It hadn't crossed my mind that he might be nervous too. He pushes his glasses up a bit as he looks out the window on my side. I've closed it. The rushing air was making my eyes water and I don't want to go into the party looking like I've been crying.

After a while, Mr. Wick turns the car into a road with big houses. They have wide, open front yards.

"What number is it again?" Mr. Wick asks over his shoulder. I look at the invitation, although I already know.

"Sixteen," I say. "Sixteen Cranberry Close."

The number out my window is twenty-seven. Mr. Wick slows the car right down, before he pulls up outside a house with white siding. Its front lawn is so neat that the grass looks painted on.

"Sixteen," Mr. Wick says. "This is it."

I wish my heart would stop beating so fast, but even Blister's hand in mine won't stop it. I let out a deep breath. I'm not sure I want to be here. I don't think I want to go in. I'd like Mr. Wick to just turn his car around before anyone sees and take us back to the safety of their house.

"We can do this," Blister says. He smiles, but his dimples hardly show.

"Sure you can," Mr. Wick says. He turns right around to look at us and leans his elbow into the seat's headrest. "You'll have a great time."

"Ready?" Blister asks.

"Ready." But I'm not. I never will be.

"OK." He starts to get out of the car, but I hold tight onto his hand and want to pull him back.

"You'll be fine, June," Mr. Wick says gently. "Blister will look out for you. I'll wait here until you're safely inside."

I look toward the house and then to Blister. I know I have to do this. It'll be OK. It might even be the beginning of things changing for the better.

I get out of the car and smooth down my skirt.

"You look great," Blister says, and he kisses my forehead.

Together, we walk up the path to the house. I hope Blister can't feel my palm sweating on his. As he knocks on the door, I look back at Mr. Wick. He waves. Blister presses his thumb onto the bell.

It's very quiet.

The door eventually opens. An old woman is standing here. Her hair is pulled back, with wisps of white breaking loose.

"Yes?" she asks.

"We're here for Cassandra's party," Blister says.

"Cassandra?"

"Yes," I manage.

"I'm sorry, you must have the wrong house."

Blister steps back and looks at the number next to the door.

"This is sixteen?" he asks.

"Yes. Sixteen Cranberry Close," she says.

"Does Cassandra live here?" I ask.

"No. Just me and Jesse, my cat."

"Sorry to disturb you," Blister says, and he pulls me away from the door and down the steps.

"But I'm sure this was the address," I say.

"It was." Blister is staring hard ahead of us. Mr. Wick is in his car, looking confused.

"I'll check the invitation," I say. "I must have read it wrong."

"You didn't," Blister says, his voice tight with anger.

"What's up?" Mr. Wick asks as we get into the back seat.

"It's the wrong address," I say, picking up the piece of paper. My name is clearly on it. And so is 16 Cranberry Close. The date is today and we're right on time.

"Is there another Cranberry Close?" I ask.

"No," Mr. Wick says. He turns to stare out the front of the car.

I look at the invitation. Maybe I've read it wrong. Maybe it got smudged. I look up at Blister for answers. He's biting the edge of his finger. His eyes look even darker.

"I don't understand," I tell him. Although I think I do.

"There is no party," Blister says quietly. I can tell that he doesn't want to say it.

"You think so?" I look up toward the silent house.

"I know so," Blister says. He's breathing loudly. He looks like he wants to thump the seat in front of him. And then he does, twice, the side of his clenched fist slamming into the headrest. I want to put my hands out to stop him. What if the girls from school are hiding and watching?

"They're losers," he says.

And I want to curl into a ball so small that they won't notice when I slide away. I'll roll into a gutter and disappear into murky water and no one will ever know.

Blister puts his arm around me and his head against mine,

but I don't want him here. The embarrassment I feel has painted every part of me with shame, and I just want to run away and never look back.

"They're not worth it," I hear Mr. Wick say from the front seat. "They're just nasty little low-lifes and you're worth a million of them."

I know it's not true, though.

And I know that on Monday I'm going to have to face them. All of them, laughing at me. Even Cassandra, who I thought was all right. Who I truly believed was being nice to me and wanting to help change things.

Mr. Wick starts the car. I keep my eyes closed and feel the motion as we turn around. I feel for the window's handle and roll it down. The sound of the car takes some of it away. The air beats on my face and pushes against my stupid, straight hair.

I quickly turn to Blister.

"I don't want to go home yet," I tell him.

"You can come to our house for as long as you want," Mr. Wick says from the front.

I can't even bear the thought of walking into their house. Tom's face all confused when we're back so early. The pity in Mrs. Wick's eyes. But I don't want to take this feeling into our trailers either. I don't want it anywhere near our place.

"OK," I say quietly.

If I had a match, I could light this humiliation and burn it up to ashes inside me.

Blister holds my hand tight, but this time nothing can make it better.

BEFORE

two months later

"Left or right?" Blister holds out his folded fists. I touch the right one and he uncurls his fingers. The jagged stone sits in his palm. "Left it is, then." He pushes up the bottom of the small bag on his back and begins to pedal.

"How's Tom?" I ask, moving my bike alongside his.

"Not great, but apparently he slept better last night."

"Can I go visit him?"

"He's coming home tomorrow."

"That's wonderful."

"With even more pills, though. He's got seven more days of these ones to keep the infection away."

"Shall we bake him something nice?" I ask.

"He'd like that." Blister reaches over to hold my hand. It makes me wobble and I laugh, but he keeps it there.

"Conjoined bikes," he says.

"That means you're stuck with me forever," I remind him.

"That wouldn't be so bad." He looks over at me, but it

makes his front wheel knock slightly into mine and he grabs both his handlebars to stop himself from falling.

"I don't think I'll be joining a circus in a hurry," he calls over his shoulder as he begins to speed away.

"Stick to being a doctor," I yell at him, pedaling hard to catch up. He's too quick, though.

I slow down and look at the fields on either side. There's a blanket of blue flowers beside me, stretching to the trees.

A car appears in the distance, getting bigger as it moves toward us. Its low hum breaks through the quiet and turns into a rush of engine as it speeds past. I hear it disappearing behind me and imagine it becoming smaller and smaller, until it's no longer there.

Blister is waiting at the crossroads.

"In your own time," he says.

"I was admiring the view," I tell him, and he smiles, his dimples dipping. "I didn't mean you," I laugh.

"Oh."

"Just the general beauty."

"So it was me, then," Blister says. I try to hit him on the shoulder, but he moves back, laughing. "Left or right." He holds his arms out straight.

"It's my turn."

"You were too late."

"That's not in the rules."

"Well, I had enough time to rewrite them."

"That doesn't seem fair to me," I say as I point to his right hand. He opens his fingers and his palm is empty.

"Right, then."

"Can we stop soon?" I ask.

"We haven't found anywhere good yet."

"Just for a break."

"How about two more stones and then if we don't see anything we'll stop."

"Deal," I say, sitting back on my bike and starting to pedal.

I've got my eyes on the next crossroads, far in the distance, when I hear music from somewhere close by. Blister is biking alongside me, but I don't think he's heard it. I slow my bike to a stop.

"What's wrong?" Blister asks, using his feet to brake.

"Can you hear it?"

"Hear what?"

"Someone's singing." We both stand still and listen.

"It's coming from over there, I reckon." Blister points to a cluster of thick, squat trees, off in the field next to us.

"Shall we see?" I ask.

"We said two more stones," Blister reminds me.

"But we found something first."

"I suppose," Blister says.

"Someone is playing guitar too."

I don't give Blister much choice. I get off my bike and push it off the road, into the bumpy field. I try not to crush too many of the wildflowers, but I know it's impossible and we can't just leave our bikes in the middle of the road.

We lay them on top of each other and walk toward the singing trees.

"It sounds like a man," I whisper. Blister nods, stepping carefully through the long grass.

It's an old man, sitting alone, his back curved against the trunk of a tree. A guitar is in his hands and sunglasses sit tight across his eyes.

I don't think he knows we're here. He's so deep in his song

that his world has shrunk to only music.

It's been too long since I've seen anyone play the guitar. The sound hurts me and I don't want it to. All I want to feel is that it's beautiful and I'm here with Blister.

"Who's there?" The music suddenly stops. The old man looks straight ahead. "Who are you?" He holds his guitar closer to him.

"Hello," Blister says, and together we walk toward him.

"We just like your music," I say. The old man's head turns toward us, but I'm sure he can't see us. "Would you keep singing?"

"How many of you are there?" he asks.

"Just two. I'm June and this is Blister."

"What sort of a name is Blister?" The old man's forehead creases. "What's your real name?"

"Jacob," Blister says.

"I'll call you that, then."

Blister looks at me and raises his eyebrows. I don't want to leave here though, not yet.

"What's your name?" I ask, sitting in the grass next to the old man.

"I don't need one," he replies.

"That's a stranger name than Blister," I say, and the man chuckles, with a sound that rattles in his throat. "Will you sing again for us?" I ask him.

"Only if you join in," he says.

Blister looks at me and shakes his head sharply.

"I'm not sure that Blister is too good," I laugh.

"Yeah," Blister says. "I'd scare the leaves off the trees."

"They're evergreen," the old man says.

"Well, I'd scare something." Blister takes off the bag from his back and sits down next to me.

"It's you and me then, June," the man says.

"I'm not so good, either," I say. I haven't really sung since my mom died. No one sings in our house anymore.

"Try," the old man says. He moves his fingers over the strings and the guitar's gentle sound fills the space between us. "You choose the song."

I look briefly at the sky.

"Carole King, 'You've Got a Friend,'" I say, before I change my mind.

"Right."

He starts to strum. And I start to sing.

I close my eyes, so that it's just me and the old man. And my mom too. Before, I couldn't remember what she sounded like, but now I can hear her so clearly in my head. Her calm, sweet voice, as she sings with me. Rocking me to sleep. Cooking together in the kitchen. Planting flowers in the yard. The music makes her live again.

The old man sings with me, his voice like smoke. And I keep going, holding my mom's voice in mine.

When we stop, the air feels empty.

I open my eyes and Blister is staring at me.

"I didn't know you could do that," he says.

"You've never sung to Jacob before?" the old man asks. I shake my head, but remember he can't see.

"No," I say.

"You have a gift," the old man says. "You should use it more."

"Do you play guitar too?" Blister asks me. He's looking confused, as though there's a whole new part of me he doesn't know.

"No." I'm looking at the old man as I reply. I want him to play again. "My mom tried to teach me a few times, but it was too difficult. Maybe I was too young."

"You should ask her to try teaching you again," the old man says. "Can she sing too?"

I know Blister is looking at me, but I don't want my mom to die here. I can make her live again, just for a bit.

"Yes," I say. "She has a beautiful voice."

"Well, when you get home," the old man says, pointing his finger in the direction of where we are, "you must go straight up and ask her to teach you."

"I will," I say.

"Is she as beautiful as you, June?" he asks.

"More so," I say. I should tell him that I'm not beautiful, that my voice has tricked him.

"You should believe in yourself. I think that Jacob believes in you, don't you, son?"

"Completely," Blister says.

The old man strums a chord and the air buzzes again. He starts to sing and I join him. This time, I keep my eyes open. This time, I watch as he rests his head back and smiles out the words. I look over at Blister and he's still staring at me. He leans over and kisses me on the lips, as I sing.

And I sing louder. To the tops of the trees and the tip of the sky. The flowers hear me. And the distant road. I mark them all with our song.

. . .

Megan is standing in my doorway. She's looking at the art project I've spread out on my bedroom floor.

"What do you want?" I ask her. These days, more than anything, she just makes me tired.

"Is that for school?" she asks. She sounds like she really is interested.

"It's none of your business."

I've painted our singing man leaning against his tree. I had to do three practice sketches before the final picture in paint. But he's ours, mine and Blister's, and I don't want her to know.

"It's good," she says, twisting her head around to get a better look.

"Close the door on your way out," I tell her. I look up and see a glimpse of hurt flash across her face. Then she seems to close up like a book.

"Do you know how ugly you are?" Her words seem young and childish, without Kathleen to drive them on.

"This is my room," I say calmly. I don't want her in here. I don't want the confusion of anger mixed with guilt that she sometimes makes me feel.

"Fine." She turns around and slams the door.

I look back down at our singing man. In the picture, I've given him eyes that see. And tomorrow after school I'll roll it up and take it to show Blister, even though I'm scared that I'll crack the paint, or crease the paper and ruin it.

The door opens suddenly. I see it too late. The orange juice that Megan throws arcs through the air before I can stop it and splashes all over my picture. The colors leak. The old man's face blurs.

"Oh, I'm so sorry," she says, kneeling down dramatically. She has a cloth and she's rubbing hard at my soaked painting, bleeding the colors and ripping the paper.

I push her back so hard that even I'm surprised. She bangs her head against the wall and screams so loudly that I want to grab the cloth and force it down her throat.

I can tell that it's my dad running up the stairs. His footsteps are loud and heavy.

"What's happened?" He goes to Megan. She's crying hysterically and trying to speak, but the words don't make sense. My dad looks at me.

"She ruined my painting," I say. I don't want to look at it.

"It was an accident," she cries.

"Hush, it's OK," my dad says, stroking her hair.

"I brought her a drink," Megan said. "But she said she didn't want it and she pushed me away. It spilled all over her picture." She's crying too much to speak again. Why can't he see that she's pretending? Acting like a child to get his sympathy.

"Where does it hurt?" my dad asks her.

"Her picture was so good," Megan says.

She buries her head in my dad's arms. He looks over the top of her at me. I can tell that he's furious.

"Look at my painting," I say, pointing down to it.

"But it wasn't Megan's fault," he says.

"I'm sorry, June." She looks at me with such innocent eyes. "I only wanted to bring you a drink."

"You did a good thing," my dad tells her.

I stare at him. I wait for him to see the truth, but I know he never will.

"It was really good," I say quietly. And Blister never got to see it.

"It's your own fault," my dad says, helping Megan to her feet. Her dramatic crying has turned to pathetic little sobs. But still he believes her. She's not even his real daughter, but still he won't see.

He shuts the door and I scream until my voice runs out. And then I rip the remains of our singing man into tiny little shreds and scatter him like raindrops over my carpet.

AFTER

"Therefore, we do not lose heart," Reverend Shaw reads. "But though our outer man is decaying, yet our inner man is being renewed day by day."

I put my hand on his Bible to stop him.

"It felt like almost everyone was trying to destroy the inner me," I say. "I tried to pretend that it didn't touch me, but it cut me inside."

"You must have felt very scared."

"And alone. The only time I felt happy was with Blister. I felt safe with him."

"Yet you never felt you could tell him everything?"

"It wasn't like that. I didn't want him to know, so that when we were together I could pretend that my other world didn't exist. I knew that if I told him, I'd never be able to escape it."

"And have you managed to escape it now?"

"No," I say. "It's part of my shadow."

"There is a way," Reverend Shaw says calmly, "because when you forgive someone you let a part of yourself go free. At the moment, the people who hurt you still have control. If you forgive them, your soul can be your own again."

"But if I do, it feels like they're getting away with it all."

"Holding on to it will only poison you. Haven't they done enough damage already?"

"Yes." My voice is so quiet that I can barely hear it.

Kathleen and Megan crowd into my mind and I don't want them there. This is my place of peace, but I don't know how to make them disappear.

"Try to let them go, June," Reverend Shaw says. "Set yourself free."

BEFORE

two months later

Blister's house is even more chaotic than normal. Everyone seems to be criss-crossing in different directions and talking loudly all at once.

"It wasn't meant to rain today," Mrs. Wick says, shoving raincoats into a big bag. She drops one and I pick it up for her.

"We won't need them," Mr. Wick says, Chubbers on his hip. "It'll stop soon and it's warm enough to dry us out."

"I'm taking them anyway." Mrs. Wick heaves the bag out the front door.

"Tom!" Mr. Wick calls up the stairs.

"Ready?" Blister asks me as he comes out of the kitchen.

I smile. "Yup."

Tom comes running down the stairs, his bare feet slapping against the wooden floor.

"Shoes, Tom." Mr. Wick is beginning to sound irritated. "And socks."

"I couldn't find any."

"I'll help him," I say, and I run up the stairs to look in the little square shelves at the top. They've each got their own place, their name carved in the wood by Mr. Wick, but the clothes still always manage to get muddled. Blister says that when it's Eddie's turn to sort, he just takes handfuls and shoves them in where they'll fit.

Tom's shelf is empty, so I pull out the clothes from Si's next to his.

"Hurry up, June!" Mr. Wick calls up the stairs.

There's one sock in Si's shelf and one in Mil's. They're slightly different sizes, but they're both blue, so they'll do.

"Coming down," I shout, as I ball them up and aim them at Tom's head. It makes him laugh when they hit him and he sits on the bottom step to put them on.

"We'll wait in the car," Mr. Wick says. "You two—" he nods to me and Blister—"will have to be in the trailer."

"But it's raining," Blister says.

"I've got the tarp covering it. You'll be fine."

"You can't do that to June," Blister protests.

"You two are the oldest without Maggie here, so if you want to come, that's where you've got to be," he says, and he walks out the front door.

"I'll be fine." I look up at Blister.

"Tom's old enough to do his own shoes," he tells me.

"I like it," I say, tightening the laces and standing up. "Let's go."

It's not raining much, but it's enough. All three of us rush to the car, where everyone is waiting, all squashed in.

Mr. Wick buckles Tom's seatbelt as Blister and I climb into the trailer and under the large sheet of gray plastic.

"And keep your heads down," Mr. Wick reminds us. He's put cushions in here for each of us, but it's still not going to be the comfiest ride.

"Sorry," Blister says, as he pulls the tarp over us.

"It's fine," I say. Because it is.

I lie down and Blister attaches the sheet to the other side. It's like we're in a little box, with light peeping through the cracks in the side.

I giggle as the car begins to pull us along, slowly at first and then gathering speed.

"It's a bit bumpy," Blister says, his voice competing with the rain.

"It's fun," I say.

"Strange idea of fun you have, June." Blister turns onto his side and looks at me.

It's amazing how everything stops when I'm this close to him, as though there's nothing else. I could live with it just being him and me forever.

He reaches over and touches my cheek. That's all there is. His skin on my skin. It's all we need.

He stares at me for such a long time. There's rain on the tarp and there's us.

"What?" I smile.

Blister takes a deep breath. "I love you, June." My breath takes in his words.

Blister loves me.

I stare at him. I can see his eyes in the semi-light.

I kiss the tips of my fingers and touch them to his lips.

"I love you too, Blister."

He puts his arms around me and pulls me so close to him. And he kisses me stronger than he's ever kissed me before.

My Blister.

My Blister, who loves me.

. . .

The car stops. I hear the doors open, but there's too much noise to work out a single conversation.

Blister unhooks the tarp. I blink in the light as the rain hits us.

"OK?" Mr. Wick asks, putting out his hand to help me jump down. I wonder if he knows how much we've been kissing. From the way he looks at Blister, I think he does.

We've parked on the side of the road, behind a long row of cars. From here we can see the edge of the fair and hear the tinny music.

"Raincoats on," Mrs. Wick says, grabbing Chubbers by the wrist as he tries to get free.

"They'll be fine," Mr. Wick says.

"It's wet." Mrs. Wick hands out the coats to the children.

Blister and I help shove arms into plastic sleeves. It's quite wet on the road and I'm beginning to wish I hadn't chosen sandals.

We walk in single file. I keep my hands on Mil's shoulders, to stop her from running among the cars.

At the entrance, Mr. Wick puts a handful of coins in the bucket. The music is louder here. And there are so many people already.

"OK, if anyone gets lost, this is the meeting place." Mr. Wick points to the pole stuck in the ground. At the top of it is a bright yellow flag. He ties a piece of string to his wrist and loops the other end through Chubbers' belt.

"Food first?" Mrs. Wick asks.

"The flying swings," Si says, pulling at Mr. Wick's coat. Eddie pushes Mil and she stumbles backwards.

"Enough, you two." Mr. Wick steps between them.

A band starts up on the stage just ahead. It's difficult to hear each other now above the blasts of trumpets and saxophones.

Tom pulls my hand.

"I'd like to see," he says. I look at Mrs. Wick.

"All right," she sighs. So we walk toward the ramshackle stage and join the small crowd at the front.

Tom wants to dance. And he wants me to dance with him, in front of all these people. He's a puppet to the music as he moves. Anyone watching would never know that, inside him, he has broken lungs. That his life will end far, far before his time.

I take his hands and swing him around. If people are looking at us, I don't care. If they're not looking, I don't care either. Because I'm making Tom laugh, I'm making him smile and I'm mending his sickness for just a bit as we stamp along to the music and clap our hands high above our heads.

Blister joins in. I've never really seen him dance before. He looks a bit awkward and he's not quite in time with the music, but I love him all the more for it. He takes Mil's hand and twists her under his arm. They link elbows and spin around. The rain keeps time with us, although it's slowing down.

We only stop when Tom gets tired, his breathing wispy in his chest.

"Let's see if we can find a table," Mr. Wick says.

"Can we go on that ride?" I ask Blister. I point to the one where the seats are climbing up and swooping low so quickly that everyone is throwing their arms up and screaming.

"Seriously?" he asks. I nod. He looks across at it, but doesn't move.

"Too scared?" I poke him in his side.

"They make me feel sick," he says.

"I'll hold your hand." I take his fingers in mine. "Please?"

"Oh, June. I hate them."

"For me."

"Go on, Blister," Tom says.

"You want to make me sick, in front of everyone?" Blister asks me.

"No. I want to go on a ride with you."

He looks at me and back at the ride.

"Dad, June wants to make me suffer."

"Good thing too," Mr. Wick says. "We can all come and watch."

Tom is pulling Blister toward the ride.

I get my purse out as we get to the barrier. The man waiting to take our money barely registers us as we step up.

"I'll pay for the pleasure of this," Mr. Wick laughs, handing the man some coins.

"Dad," Blister says pleadingly.

"Enjoy."

I take Blister's hand and pull him toward two seats. We snap belts across our laps and the man comes to pull down a bar to trap us in.

"I really hate this, June."

"I really love you, Blister."

I swing my legs as we wait. A younger child gets onto the seat in front of us. I wave as we begin to move.

The ride starts slowly. I put my hand on top of Blister's as the seat climbs up and starts to rush down the other side. It's going faster than I imagined it would. Blister's family is there and then they're gone. Steeply up. Quicker. They're there. Gone.

Blister's eyes are shut. His fingers are curled around the bar. He's hating it. And I made him do this for me. The guilt suddenly whips at me with the wind.

"I'm sorry," I shout, but I don't think he hears me above the thudding music and the noise of his own fear.

They're there, laughing. They're gone.

Fast up. My stomach ducking and clinging to the top.

I look across the heads of the people and suddenly I see them—a cluster of girls from Megan's class. They're close enough to spot me, but they're walking away.

The ride goes straight down.

When we go up again, I look to where they were, but they've disappeared.

We begin to slow. Blister's family is laughing, but his eyes are shut too tight to see.

"I'm sorry." This time, he can hear me.

"It's my fault," he says. "I shouldn't have gotten on."

"I won't make you do anything you don't want again," I promise him as the ride crawls to a stop.

"Never?"

"Never." I kiss him on the cheek. I don't tell him that I'm nervous now, that maybe we've been seen. He doesn't look at me as we step down, my blood still spinning.

. . .

The table in the food tent has two small benches free. Mrs. Wick sits down with Tom, and the others pile on and squish together. Chubbers is put in the middle of the table.

"Hot dogs all around?" Mr. Wick asks.

"I'll come and help," I say. Blister doesn't look like he wants to eat. I've done this to him.

"You'll feel better in a moment." Mrs. Wick reaches up and pats his arm.

"I'll be fine," he says, but I know we both want to rewind time.

As I wait in line with Mr. Wick, I try not to glance around. If I don't see the girls from school, then I can pretend that they're not here.

"Shame your family couldn't join us," he says to me.

"Yes." I look away. I don't want him to bring Kathleen in here.

"What were they up to?"

"They're busy. My dad says maybe next time," I lie.

"You should bring them over one day. It seems wrong that we've never met them."

"That'd be good," I lie again.

I won't say that Blister is still my secret, that his name has never been mentioned in my house. And that I'll never let them know. One day, I'll run away with my boyfriend and I won't come back and they won't know where to look for me.

"Blister doesn't tell us much. Just that you're not so close to Kathleen and Megan. Is that right?"

"I suppose." We step forward, closer to the till.

"It seems a shame. To only have one sister and not get along."

"She's not really my sister."

"I thought she was your dad's daughter?" We move again and Mr. Wick takes two trays from the shelf and passes one to me. "Shows how much I pay attention." He laughs lightly, before he leans toward the woman behind the counter. "Nine hot dogs, please."

The woman smiles. "Big family?"

"Big enough." Mr. Wick laughs again.

I watch as my tray is piled with food, and the word *sister* burrows its way somewhere deep where I don't want it to go.

I stand next to the table with Blister, and I watch as Mr. Wick measures out Tom's medicine and he drinks it up. He's definitely more listless than earlier and I see Mr. and Mrs. Wick look at each other quickly when he starts to cough. But they hand out the hot dogs and Tom smiles as he bites into his, ketchup squeezing out the sides of the bun.

I still don't like eating in front of Blister's family. They never say anything, but I know what they must think.

I want to tell them. I want them to know that me being a bit overweight isn't my fault. That I don't want to eat everything that Kathleen puts in front of me but fear makes me do what she says. And that the older I get, the further away my dad seems to go and the less he can see. I wipe the mustard from my mouth. Blister is folding his empty napkin into smaller and smaller squares.

"Did you know, you can't fold paper more than twelve times?" he says.

"I've folded one fourteen times," Eddie says. Blister raises his eyebrows as he glances at him.

"Really?"

Mrs. Wick wipes Chubbers' hands. "Where to next?" she asks no one in particular.

"There's livestock judging at two thirty." Mr. Wick lifts Mil from the bench. "So why don't we look at the stalls for a bit?" He grabs on to the string attached to Chubbers before he can run away.

"Can I win something for Maggie?" Tom asks.

"You can try," Mr. Wick says.

"She'd love that," I say. I take his hand and Blister stacks up the trays and takes them away.

Outside the tent, the rain has stopped. The sky is still muddy, but for now it's dry.

Tom needs me to walk slowly. I don't like the way his breathing sounds.

"You OK?" I ask. He looks up at me and nods. "Are you hurting at all?" He shakes his head.

"Please," Si whines, and we all stop at the coconut toss.

"OK. But that'll be it for you," Mr. Wick says. "Are you sure you want to spend it on this?"

Si screws up his nose.

"This'll be easier." Mrs. Wick points to the fishing ducks on the other side of us.

"You could do this one, Tom," I say. The children are already grabbing rods and I help Tom squeeze into the middle so he can pick one too.

Blister isn't with us, though. I see him pass money to the man at the coconut toss and he's given three wooden balls. He glances over at me and holds them high, smiling.

He misses with every single one.

I'm laughing when he comes back to me.

"I wanted to win you something," he says. I think his pride might be hurt, just a little bit.

"I don't mind," I tell him.

"June, I've got one!" Tom shouts. At the end of his hook is a duck. I reach over to help him hold it straight and we pull it back to take the plastic animal from the end. Underneath it is a red sticker. "Have I won?" He starts to cough. His whole body shakes and he holds on to my arm as he folds over.

Mrs. Wick passes Chubbers to Blister and she kneels down so that Tom can sit on her legs. I hate watching him hurting so much. I hate that people are looking over and there's nothing we can do.

"I think we'll get you home," Mrs. Wick says gently. Tom looks up at her.

"But I won a prize," he says weakly.

"We'll get your prize."

"It's a red sticker," I say to the man, as I pass him Tom's duck. He reaches for a tray and holds it close to the edge.

"You can choose one thing from in here," the man says, glancing over his shoulder to watch the boys who've arrived on the other side.

Mrs. Wick holds Tom up. There are cards, wands and swords, but he reaches for something in the middle. It's a big ring, with a plastic green heart set in its center.

He passes it to me. "Is it for Maggie?" I ask.

"It's for you," he smiles, but his fragile lungs make him cough again. He doubles over on his mom's lap as her hands gently hit his back to help him breathe more easily.

"Time to go," Mr. Wick says.

And none of the children complain. Mrs. Wick picks up Tom and we weave in and out of the happy crowd toward the car.

Blister holds my hand. In my other palm, I hold my little heart ring tightly.

. . .

On Monday morning, the whispers start at the back of the classroom.

"June's got a boyfriend. June's got a boyfriend."

I thought I had been lucky at the fair and they hadn't seen me.

Someone throws a ball of rolled-up paper at me. It hits my arm and falls to the floor.

"June's got a boyfriend." The taunting is getting louder as more people join in.

"How did you manage that?" Ryan walks up, puts his hands on my desk and leans his breath into me. It feels like every person in the room is laughing at me.

I try to make their words roll away.

Cherry walks up and puts a scrappy picture in front of me. It's a drawing of a boy with glasses. They've made him ugly, which he isn't, and they've given him pimples. They haven't drawn his beautiful smile and his deep dimples. It's not Blister at all.

"I might've guessed he'd need glasses," Cherry says. I want to say something nasty back, but nothing comes.

I watch as she walks away from me. I imagine sticking knives into her back and watching the blood leak onto her lily-white shirt. She's still walking, but I want her crumpled on the floor.

The boys sitting at the front circle their fingers over their eyes and kiss the air.

Yes. I want to tell them. *Yes, I have a boyfriend. He's called Blister and he's beautiful.*

But I know Blister is telling me to stay quiet. Breathe. Count to ten.

"Does everyone hate him, too?" Ryan whispers in my ear. I so nearly hit him. But Blister stops me. *Don't do it, June.* I stare out the window and imagine him standing there. And I smile as Mr. Jennings walks into the classroom to start the lesson.

· · ·

After school, I bike to our trailers. Two paper dragonflies are perched on the gate. One is blue, one is purple. Their wings have been carefully cut into lines of thin veins. Each one could fit into the palm of my hand. I'm sure that they're talking to each other, deep in conversation about something I can't hear.

I touch the blue one. It's only attached with thin wire and I make it tilt back too far. I try to straighten it, but I'm worried I'll break its wing.

I climb over the gate carefully. The aster flowers at the edge of the path are beginning to dry up and die.

Blister is asleep on a blanket outside our school trailer. His head is tipped to the side and his breathing makes his chest go up and down. I want to put my hand there and feel the beating of his heart, but I don't want to wake him.

Next to him is one of his thick, heavy books, its medical words face down on the grass.

I go quietly into the art room. The day's heat is still in here, but it's much cooler than it would be at midday.

On the floor are tiny lines of blue and purple. The dragonflies' veins.

I pick up some sheets of paper and a pair of scissors and take them back to the blanket outside. Blister hasn't moved. He has a little frown wriggled on his forehead, even though he's sound asleep. I almost push my thumb there, to iron it out, but I stop myself.

I start to fold a piece of paper. I have to cut it to shape it. I fold it again and then undo it and rub it flat. I've already ruined it, so I crumple it up and take up another one.

I'm more careful, but I mess it up again. I wanted to give

it to Blister, but I end up slamming the scissors sharp into the ground.

I must make too much noise, because Blister wakes up. He opens his eyes and leans on his elbow.

"Hey," he says.

"Hey yourself."

"Did I fall asleep?"

"Looks that way."

"You OK?" He sits up properly and puts his hands on my knees.

"Yes," I lie. And he knows it. I let my shoulders slump down. "I'm unhappy, Blister, and I don't want to be."

"Did you see our dragonflies?"

Oh, Blister.

"Yes," I say. "They're beautiful. Thank you."

He leans forward and kisses me. And I kiss him back.

Kissing Blister makes all the rest just dissolve and disappear. Blister, me; me, Blister.

I don't know life before him. I don't want life after him. I don't know where I start and he ends.

We stay on the blanket, until the sun moves far enough to make the trees' shadow creep over us.

I want to stay here forever, but I know I have to go.

. . .

At the weekend, I escape again to Blister's house. No one is in the hallway, but through the window at the end I can see them in the backyard. Their shouts stop at the glass.

I stand and watch them. In the frame, Mr. Wick is carrying a bucket, then he disappears out of view. No one is there now. And then Mil runs quickly to the other side. Blister walks across the path, carrying a pole.

I go through the kitchen and out the back door, into the sunshine.

"June!" Tom comes running up. "We're having our own fair."

"Hold it straight," Mr. Wick yells, and he turns on the faucet by the wall. Eddie is holding the hose at the other end and water gushes from it into the bucket. "Say when," Mr. Wick calls.

"When!" Eddie shouts. He's hopping from one foot to the other on the grass.

"June, can you grab a chair from inside?" Mrs. Wick calls. Blister turns to me and smiles.

In the kitchen, I pick up the nearest chair and go back outside. Blister takes it from me. He puts it down and gives me a hug that melts my bones.

"We're recreating the bits we missed at the fair," he says.

"One more chair, June," Mrs. Wick says. She's standing in the middle of the lawn, holding a long bamboo stick.

I run into the house and get another. Between us, we balance the stick on the two chairs to make the final jump. It looks a bit tall for the little ones to get over, but they can roll underneath.

By the flowerbed, Mr. Wick has balanced a shelf on a bench. Tom is piling up the empty tin cans, but he can't reach high enough for the top ones and they keep falling off the back.

Blister and I go to help him. We have to level the shelf a bit so that the cans sit straight. I lift Tom up to put the top few on. He's so light, even though he's tall enough for his feet to almost touch the ground.

Mr. Wick blows a whistle sharply.

"Evan," Mrs. Wick says, "too loud." He blows it again so softly that we can hardly hear it and exaggerates tiptoes as we all follow him to the end of the lawn.

"Right, first up, we have the horse jumping." He picks up an old bicycle horn from the grass and squeezes its rubber end.

"How are you going to time us?" Si asks.

"You're all going together," Mr. Wick says.

"But they'll crash into each other," Mrs. Wick says.

"They'll be fine." He grins and pats Chubbers on the head as he looks at me. "The oldest ones will go backwards."

"That's not fair," Blister laughs.

"It's the rules," Mr. Wick says. "Right, all of you have to start behind this line." We all huddle back, behind the stretch of sweaters on the grass. "Ready?"

I tuck the ends of my skirt into my underwear, quickly take off my sandals and throw them to the side.

"I'll be better with bare feet," I say.

"Extra points for style," Mr. Wick says.

"Jump high," Blister tells me as we turn our backs to the course.

"Go!" shouts Mr. Wick, sounding the bicycle horn.

But Blister grabs me around the waist.

"That's cheating," I yell, and struggle free.

At the first post I spin in the air. "More points for me," I shout.

Blister grabs my hand and there's chaos as we all stumble over the rest of the balancing bamboos and I run last over the finish line.

Eddie and Si start bickering about who came first.

"Can we have something a bit calmer now?" asks Mrs.

Wick, picking up Chubbers and brushing his knees clean. "Apple bobbing?"

"Yes!" Tom says, and he pushes me toward the two buckets on the corner of the lawn.

"OK, line up in two teams, one behind each bucket," Mr. Wick says. "You've got to keep your hands behind your backs, and when you've got an apple in your mouth, drop it onto the grass and it'll be the next person's turn."

Blister stands opposite me in his line.

"I'm watching you," he says.

"Bring it on," I reply, pushing up imaginary sleeves.

We chant the name of each person. Mil takes ages and Mrs. Wick eventually scoops one up and puts it in her mouth.

Blister already has his head in the bucket when it's my turn. His hands hold the sides. His hair is soaked. Water runs down the back of his T-shirt.

"June—" Tom pushes me forward—"your turn." His face is beaming. His cheeks are full of color and his eyes are full of life.

"Having fun?" I ask.

He nods. "Quick."

I kneel on the wet grass, put my hands on the bucket, take a deep breath and lean my head forward into the water.

Instantly, Kathleen is here. She's holding me down. She's filled the kitchen sink and has me kneeling on a chair. She pushes my head in and holds it until my breath is running out. I thrash out with my arms, but she won't let me up. I swallow water and start to cough, but still her hands hold me under. I kick so hard that the chair falls away.

Someone is pulling me back.

"You're OK," Blister says. I can't get enough air, but the water has gone. "I've got you," he says gently.

We're sitting on the grass. I open my eyes and they're all staring at me. Wide, innocent eyes, wondering what happened to June.

"OK," Mr. Wick says. He moves them away and glances briefly at Mrs. Wick. "We'll break for lunch. After that, we'll do the coconut toss."

Tom looks back over his shoulder at me as they all huddle into the house.

The sun tries to dry me while Blister strokes my hair. But in my memory I haven't escaped. I'm still drowning.

. . .

Blister and I eat alone in the yard. We move slightly into the shade. The lawn is scattered with toppled chairs, bamboo sticks and apples. Through the kitchen's open window, we can hear his family. They're laughing and shouting. I've forgotten what it's like to laugh in my home. What it's like to have a mom who lights up when she's with you.

"Why did your parents have so many children?" I ask.

"Because they wanted us."

"Because they wanted to give you all a home, or they just wanted lots of kids?"

"A bit of both, I think."

"Will they adopt more?"

"I don't think so. I think they're done."

"What if someone really needed them? How are they going to say no?"

"They have to. Mom's exhausted now. At some point, if you don't stop, you're doing the wrong thing for the kids you already have."

"I suppose."

"If you haven't got the time and energy to look after them, then there's no point saving them in the first place."

I feel crushed. Because my dad has the time and energy to save me, but he's blind to it.

"Would you adopt?" Blister asks me.

"I don't know. I've never really thought about having children." What if I end up like Kathleen?

"I want lots," Blister says. "Maybe not seven, but definitely a lot."

Si comes rushing out from the kitchen.

"Can June do the coconut toss now?" he asks, holding a tennis ball high above his head.

"Just me?" I ask.

"Yes," Blister replies, standing up. He puts his hand out to pull me up too.

The rest of his family spills from the house and gathers around me at the bench piled high with empty tin cans.

Si gives me the ball.

"Why only me?" I ask, looking questioningly at Blister.

"Because if you knock them all off," he says, "you get a prize." I raise my eyebrows at him and he laughs. "Stand back, everyone. Give the top can crasher some space."

The children all step back.

"Aim carefully," Tom says.

I swing my arm and throw the ball. Half the cans clatter to the ground, leaving a sort of jagged triangle.

"Not bad," Blister says.

"But I don't get my prize."

"I didn't say you had to do it with one shot. Just that you have to knock them all off."

"Oh. That's easy," I say. It takes two more throws before I dislodge the final can and the shelf is empty. "Ta-da." I bow to the crowd.

Blister walks to the flower bed behind the bench. He reaches next to a rock and comes back with a little paper bag.

"I didn't manage to win you anything at the real fair. So I got you this." He's suddenly awkward. "It's an early birthday present."

"He couldn't wait until tomorrow," Mrs. Wick laughs.

Chubbers claps his hands and jumps from foot to foot.

"Open it," Mil urges me.

"Give her a bit of space!" Mr. Wick says, trying to move them all back a bit.

"It's OK," I say.

I open the bag. It's a necklace, with a tiny compass at the end.

"It's a locket," Blister says. "It opens." Inside is a bit of chipped stone with "L or R?" written above it.

I stay so still, staring at it.

"Do you like it?" Blister asks.

"I love it," I say.

"Shall I put it on you?" he asks.

I nod.

Blister closes the compass and holds it in place. I turn away from him, so he can clasp it. I can feel it against my skin. I reach my fingers up to touch it.

Blister bends down and kisses me gently.

"You'll never get lost now," he smiles.

BEFORE

one week later

"I was with Jennifer and Helen at Creekend Pool," I lie, remembering instead Blister and me side by side on the grass, our feet flat against the outside wall of our trailer.

I push the creamy potato around my plate. Kathleen never gives me so much when my dad is here, but I still don't want to eat it.

"I was there, too," Megan says, "with Emily. But I didn't see you."

"I didn't see you, either," I say. I put the food in my mouth so that I don't have to say anymore.

"Emily said that Bell Farm Fair was really fun," Megan says, looking at my dad. But I know she's talking to me. It was her friends who spotted me there with Blister and his family. "We should go next year."

I can hear Kathleen eating. There's the scrape of the cutlery against the plate and her mouth chewing her food. It's one of my worst sounds in the world. It makes me feel sick. She swallows her mouthful.

"You won't get me going on one of those rides," Dad laughs.

"June's got some news," Megan says. She's smiling, as though she's my friend.

"Oh?" But he doesn't sound that interested as he puts a big forkful of shredded green beans into his mouth. I get the feeling that my dad's given up on me. That he has no energy left to unravel the mess that I've become. It makes me want to shout that maybe I've given up on him too. I don't think he's even thought of that, or that he even cares.

"You should tell them," Megan says. I look at her, as if I don't understand. But I think I do. I'm sure I know what she's going to say.

"You tell us, then," Kathleen urges her, prodding her arm playfully with the end of her fork.

"June's got a boyfriend," Megan says.

Dad stares at me, surprised. And it's almost worth hearing it, to see the look on Kathleen's face. Yet, inside, I'm terrified. Blister is my secret. My precious thing that I never want them to know, never want them to touch. But now he's at the threshold to our house and Megan is going to drag him in.

"No, I don't," I say.

"Yes, you do," Megan says, putting the smallest mouthful of potato into her nasty, little mouth. "It's great, June. Don't be embarrassed about it."

"Honey, it's wonderful," Kathleen says. She leans right over and squeezes my hand.

"You didn't tell me," my dad says.

"Because it's not true," I lie.

"So that's where you've been sneaking off to," Kathleen laughs. "You've been with a boy."

"No, I haven't."

"So you've been lying about where you've been?" My dad looks hurt, rather than angry.

If you hadn't stopped paying attention to me, maybe I would have told you, I want to yell at him. *You should have noticed. You should already know.*

"What's his name?" Kathleen asks, her voice like a child. "You could invite him over. We could do a lunch."

Megan looks at me. I can see triumph behind that smile, but my dad just can't see it. Or won't.

"You know I haven't got a boyfriend, Megan," I say, more loudly than I'd intended. "You're being cruel."

My dad turns to her. *Really look at her, Dad. Please see.*

"Why would Megan say that?" is all he asks.

"Maybe she's hiding her own boyfriend," I say.

I can tell that I've got them. They don't know who to believe. I have a flicker of power for the first time. I hold it with both hands.

"Megan?" Kathleen asks. A red blush creeps up Megan's white skin. "Do you have a boyfriend?" Megan looks like she might cry. I don't feel any pity, not even a tiny drop.

"No," she says.

"You girls," my dad laughs. "I can't keep up with you."

And I think I've won.

. . .

I know she's following me. I thought she would, as soon as I saw her looking at me like that when I left the house. I stop my bicycle and hear the car stop. I start again and its engine starts up. I won't look behind me. I have to pretend that I don't know.

I do a big detour, cutting off way before our trailers, so that Kathleen doesn't go anywhere close. I loop back and end up at the edge of the river path by our house. Cars can't come down here.

I pedal quickly on the stony ground, around the corner and out of sight.

I haven't come here for months. I like to see my mom's heron, but I hate that it's at the spot where she died. Where they dragged her lifeless body from the river.

And my dad replaced her with Kathleen.

Not long, Blister always says. *Soon, you'll be free.*

I slow my bike as I see the heron, sitting looking at the water. My mom loved it here. There were nicer places to swim, with clearer water, but she liked it here. She said dark things made her feel safer.

But then it killed her.

There's a noise behind me. I turn round and she's here.

"So, you've been coming here," Kathleen laughs. "No boyfriend after all." She walks out from among the trees. Instinctively, I step back, although she's not close enough to touch me. "Just like your mom, an ugly little duckling. But then one of the ugly little ducklings drowned."

"She wasn't ugly," I say. I want to kill her.

"That's not what your father says." Her smile burns me. But I lock myself down. I try to put up a shield so high that her words can't find a way in.

"He'd never say that about my mom."

"Wouldn't he? He thinks I'm far prettier than she ever was. And he thinks that Megan is far prettier than you."

"I don't care what you say about Megan. He'll always love me more than her."

"Will he?"

"Yes. He's my dad," I tell her.

"And he shouldn't favor one daughter over another, should he?"

"Megan's not his daughter."

"Maybe you don't know everything," she says calmly.

Her look makes my stomach turn over.

Then she smiles at me and before I can stop her she picks up my mom's heron. She yanks it hard from its wooden pole in the ground.

"No," I try to say. She steps back and swings it violently against a tree. There's a loud crack. She swings it again and the heron begins to splinter. Again, and it's cracked in two.

There are voices on the path. Kathleen drops my mom's broken heron on the grass.

"Oh, June," she says. "What have you done?"

Slowly, she walks away. Her blonde hair is swallowed by the trees.

• • •

I stay with Blister in our trailer until late in the evening. I've never missed supper before, without telling my dad where I am. But now I'm sixteen, maybe I can do what I want.

I imagine them all sitting at the kitchen table, eating in silence, glancing at the clock. Or maybe they've barely noticed I'm not there. They're talking happily about their day, Kathleen spooning more lamb onto my dad's plate. Megan in the middle of them both.

Blister and I lie on the cushions in our art room. We're playing thumb wars, but I'm barely pressing down on his hand at all.

"Are you sure everything's all right, June?" he asks, holding my hand gently. I nod, because my thoughts are too complicated to find words for. I don't even understand them myself. What was Kathleen trying to tell me? About my dad? About Megan?

"Then you're going to have to go home," he says.

"I could stay here."

"You can't."

"They'd never know where I was."

"Precisely," Blister says. "Your dad won't know where you are and he'll be worried."

"He's given up caring."

"No, he hasn't. He never will."

"He has. He's not interested in anything about me anymore. He prefers Megan to me."

"That's not true, June. You're his daughter. You'll always come first."

I think Megan might be his daughter too.

"Come on." Blister gets up and straightens his T-shirt. He puts out his hand to help me up. "I need to get home. I'm starving and Mom will start to wonder where I am."

"Can I come back to your house?" *Please, Blister, please.*

"You've got to go home."

He takes my hand and we close the door and walk down the steps.

At the gate, Blister kisses me. I try to make it last longer, but he pushes me gently away.

"Come on," he says. "It's getting dark."

He picks up my bike from where it leans against his and I take it from him.

How can I feel so lonely when he's standing here, right

next to me? But it's a feeling so deep, so real, that it makes my veins ache.

"I love you," he says, and I know he means it.

"I love you, too."

"You'll be fine, June," he tells me. I nod and swing my bike around. I don't look back at him as I pedal off.

I stop when I'm halfway home and unclasp my compass locket. I tuck it safely into the pocket of my shorts. They still don't know. They don't know about Blister. Megan tried, but she failed.

I nearly don't go home, but I know I have to. The front door is open. Quietly, I go up the path and put my bike along the side of the house. Megan sees me through the kitchen window as I walk back. Relief sweeps over her face.

"June!" I hear her cry.

My dad rushes out the door, with Kathleen and Megan behind him.

"Where've you been?"

"We were so worried," Kathleen says. Her spindly arms are around me. I want to vomit into her sweet-smelling hair. I have to push her away.

"June." My dad's voice is tipping into anger.

"Can I go to my room?" I ask.

"Where were you?" he demands.

"Just out," I tell him. I don't even want to look at him.

"You were clearly out. But where?"

"I biked down to Laurel's Corner," I lie. "I lost track of time."

"Have you eaten?" Kathleen asks as my dad ushers us all into the house.

"Yes." The lies for her are so easy.

"I'm glad you're back," Megan says. I won't look at her.

"You can't just stay out," my dad says. "You need to let us know."

"OK," I say. I lean against the banister, facing away from them all.

"You don't seem to care that we were worried." My dad's voice is getting louder. *Don't pretend that you're worried*, I want to shout. "June?"

Kathleen moves and I think she puts her hand on his arm.

"Bradley," she says gently, "she's back now. That's all that matters."

"It's not all that matters," my dad says sharply.

"Well, let's talk about it another day. I'm sure June won't do it again. Will you, honey?"

"No," I say. *Maybe*. And I walk away from them, up the stairs and to my room.

. . .

I'm woken in the night by the door opening. Whoever is in here closes it softly behind them. I hear them walking across the carpet. I think it's only one of them. The breathing is so quiet. Is it Kathleen?

I lie still. I pretend to be asleep, but my heart is beating loudly in my ears.

Someone touches the bed. They are at the end, by my feet. A hand pats the bed-covers, closer toward me. They're touching my arm, my shoulder. The hand is on my face.

I keep myself turned to the wall. I am asleep. They will go.

But they feel for my hair. It's gripped back gently from my scalp.

There's the sound of scissors cutting through it.

I don't move.

They're going away. The breathing is disappearing. I hear the bedroom door opening. Closing. They're gone.

I stay, staring at the wall, my eyes open now.

I don't want to feel what they've done. I don't want to know. I'm asleep and it's a dream.

But my hands go to my head. The hair on one side is jagged. I feel numb.

I get out of bed and turn on my light. I don't want to look in the mirror here, not in my bedroom.

I open my door and walk down the hall to the bathroom. The fan whirs on as I pull the light cord.

Above the sink is the mirror. And I see me.

She has cut a big chunk of my hair, almost to the scalp. Beneath the shards, you can see my skin. On the other side, my hair is splayed out from sleep. It's long, almost to my shoulder. Corkscrew curls that Blister always says he likes.

But on one side they're gone.

I pull open the cupboard underneath the sink. Beneath the new tubes of toothpaste and rolls of toilet tissue, I find some nail scissors.

Myself looks at me from the mirror. Maybe this is a dream. Maybe I don't have to do this.

I start to cut into the remaining curls. Wrapping lines of my hair in my fist, I hold the scissors and slice through it. It's difficult, working with my reflection. I have to be careful not to cut my hand.

I hear someone walking down the hall. My dad is in the doorway and he can't hide the horror on his face.

"June?" He doesn't try to stop me. "What are you doing?"

I don't answer him. Instead, I do the final cut, open my hand and let the hair fall like maple seeds to the tiled floor.

"Why?" I haven't seen him cry since my mom died, but his voice is beginning to crack and he looks like he's on the edge.

"I'm tired," I tell him. "I want to go to bed."

"June." My dad reaches out for me. I want to go to him. I want him to know. I want him to save me. But I'm not sure I even know who he is anymore.

I brush past him and rush back to my room.

. . .

"Don't you like it?" I hold my head high and talk directly at Megan. "I did it myself." She looks so stunned that she doesn't speak.

Kathleen turns and does a fake little gasp.

"Your hair," she whispers.

"Yes. I wanted a change." I go to the table and pick an apple out of the fruit bowl. "I'm going out. I won't need breakfast."

"But I've done pancakes," Kathleen says. I don't bother to answer her. Instead, I walk away, out of the kitchen and out the front door.

I pedal fast, laughing hysterically. She tried to break me, but she didn't. I showed her that I'm too strong. That I don't care what she does, because she'll never win.

But the feeling completely disappears as I get closer to Blister's home. In an instant, it bursts and is gone.

I look ugly. My hair is gone and Blister won't want me. A single butterfly beats hard in me. It's taking up all the space, right up to my throat.

But still I keep going. I won't let her win.

I lean my bicycle against their hedge. The front door is open, as always. I don't call out. I want the house to be empty. I don't want anyone to see.

In the kitchen, Mrs. Wick is cutting oranges on the chopping board. She turns when she hears me come in and I see her smile freeze.

"June," she says softly.

I don't know what to say. Anything will be a lie. I wouldn't have chosen to look like this.

"Is Blister here?" I ask.

"I think he's still in bed." Mrs. Wick holds the knife in mid-air. "Is everything all right?" she asks.

"Yes," I reply, and leave her alone.

Blister's room is almost dark. He has heavy curtains covering his window and they barely let any of the morning light in. I go quietly to the outline of his bed, pull up the corner of his blanket and slide myself in beside him.

He wakes up slowly. He must be confused. I've never been in his bed before.

"Hey," he says sleepily. He turns and puts his arm over my stomach.

"Hey, you," I reply. I'm surrounded by the smell of him, like a blanket.

He starts to kiss me, stronger than he's done before. His hands are over the top of my T-shirt. I kiss him back. This way, everything is OK. We can stay like this and he'll never know.

"I've never kissed you so early in the morning," he says. In the darkness, I know he smiles. I feel it in every part of me. This is where I want to be, forever.

Blister kisses my cheek. He touches my hair. And he pulls back, as I knew he would.

He reaches over me. There's the sound of his hand on the chair by his bed, a string being pulled and a soft click.

It's so bright I instinctively duck my eyes. When I open them and blink in the light, Blister has already put on his glasses and he's staring at me.

"What have you done to your hair?" he asks. He hates it.

I want to fade into the darkness and never come back.

He touches my head. His fingers are soft on my scalp.

"I didn't do it," I say quietly. Realization crosses Blister's face.

"Did she do this to you?" He starts to breathe quickly and there's an anger in his eyes I've never seen before.

I feel the tears come and I'm too tired to fight them. I let them own me. I curl myself into the smallest I can go and they shake me hard. My tears wet Blister's sheet, but I don't stop them.

He holds me tight as I weep. Deep, deep tears that I've hidden for so long.

Blister kisses my ruined hair.

And he doesn't say a word. He just keeps his arms strong around me and lets me cry.

My throat hurts, my chest hurts, my heart hurts.

I want to scream, but I have nothing left.

When I'm still, when I'm quiet, Blister turns me to look at him.

"Are you telling me everything, June?"

I don't blink; I don't breathe. There are too many years of things left unsaid, and if I begin to tell him now, I'm terrified that my mind will unravel and it'll never stop.

"I need to tell my parents that Kathleen did this to you," he says.

"No." I shake my head.

"They can help you."

"No."

"Please, June."

"I can deal with it," I tell him.

"Are you worried they won't believe you?" he asks. "Because they will." *Will they? Will anyone?*

"Soon I won't have to be there anymore," I say.

"My parents won't judge you. They'll help you."

"No." I pull myself up so that I'm sitting on his pillow, my back against the wall. "Promise me you won't, Blister."

I know he's hurting too and I know what I'm asking him. But soon I'll be free. It's easier this way.

I hold his face in my hands.

"Please, promise me."

He sighs, heavily. But then he says what I need.

"I promise."

. . .

I feel naked, sitting at the Wicks' kitchen table. Even though Si seems to have forgotten my short hair already, I keep catching Blister looking at me.

"It's kind of cheating," Si says. It's only us and Blister sitting here. Everyone else is scattered around the house. Through the window, I can see Mr. Wick in the backyard with Tom, fixing a new swing onto a tree.

I count the triangle toast lined up in the metal rack on the table. Eight pieces left. They're like shark fins dotted down a backbone.

"But I never call it origami." Blister rips off a corner of toast with his teeth.

"You still shouldn't use glue," Si says.

What if he was Megan's dad, too? I want to ask Blister. I want him to tell me that I've got it all wrong. Instead, I try to force my thoughts away.

Through the glass, Mr. Wick balances Tom on the small plank of wood. I watch as he yanks at the rope to test it and Tom nods and looks up at the branches.

"Do you want me to teach you how to do it, or not?" Blister asks.

Si picks up his glass of milk and slowly drinks it. The line of white moves lower down the glass.

"I want you to," he finally says.

"Then quit complaining," Blister says. "Or whatever it is you're doing."

"Can we do a dragon?" Si asks.

"Try doing that without glue," Blister says, shoving back his chair as he stands up. He carries his plate in one hand to the dishwasher, his last bit of toast in the other. "You going to come, June?"

He's looking at me differently. I know he is. It must be like looking at an ugly stranger.

"I'm going out to see Tom," I say. Blister glances out the window.

"OK." He seems awkward, as though he doesn't quite know how to be with me.

I'm still here, Blister. It's still me.

The back door is open. Outside, it feels unsettled. The warm sits on my skin, but doesn't quite go in.

Tom is alone on the swing, staring at the sky. He hears me walking across the grass, and when he sees me he can't hide that he's shocked.

"You've cut your hair."

"Yes." I almost touch it, but I don't. If I can't feel it, I can pretend it doesn't look so bad. Maybe it's longer than the mirror told me.

"I prefer it long," Tom says.

"So do I."

"Will you grow it again?"

"Do you want me to?"

"Yes."

"Then I will," I say.

He smiles at me, but he looks sad. There's a silence surrounding him on the swing, like his thoughts are circling and they're not happy.

"Shall I push you?" I ask. Tom screws up his nose a bit. "You're never too old to be pushed on a swing."

I walk around behind him and carefully pull the wooden seat high. Tom would normally laugh, but he's silent.

"Hold tight," I say, and I let him go. He swings down and up the other side, his toes tipping up to the sky.

I push it again and Tom swings higher. And again. It releases something in me, as I swing my arms and push the seat as high as it can go. The branch above us creaks slightly, but I don't stop. It's taking a bit of my anger with it and I'm beginning to feel free.

"It's too high, June," Tom says.

I grab the ropes and slow the swing down. Tom's feet scuff the ground.

"Shall I spin you?" I ask, but Tom doesn't answer. I walk around to the front of him. His face is still, but big tears are falling down his cheeks.

"Tom." I kneel down in front of him and put my hands over his. "What is it?"

He just looks at me, wide-eyed, crying silently. I want to make it all better—I want to take away his sadness, but I don't know what to do.

"Do you think the swing will take my weight too?" I ask. The branch above us looks strong. Tom nods and I help him up, so that I can sit down and he can sit on my lap. He's too big for it, really, but he's so light. I hold my arms across him and hug him to me.

The ropes stretch, but I don't think the branch will break.

I push my feet on the ground, so that we're moving, just a bit.

"Do you still have the ring I gave you?" Tom asks quietly.

"Of course. It's one of my most special things. So it's in my most special things box." Tucked away, where no one else can see.

"What else is in there?"

"Just best things. A paper angel Blister made me. And a paper tulip and a dried arrowhead flower. I keep my compass necklace in there, when I'm not wearing it. And a scarf of my mom's. When I really miss her, I take it out and smell it. If I close my eyes, I can imagine she's in the same room as me."

"Do you miss her a lot?"

"Sometimes," I say.

And suddenly Tom starts to cry again. He's louder now. Real unhappiness is cracking up from his throat. It breaks my heart to hear him.

"It's OK, Tomski," I say, and I hold him tight. I let him cry. I don't tell him to stop. I want the hurt to go out of him.

We both wipe the tears from his cheeks.

"I'm scared," he whispers.

"Why?"

Tom looks up at me. "Because I'm going to die."

His words hit into me, one by one.

"We're all going to die." I squeeze him so tight. There's nothing else I can do. No magic hope. He's going to die before all of us and the thought crushes my heart.

"But I don't want to die the way I know I will," he says. "I'll be really hurting and they'll have to help me breathe."

"Maybe it won't be like that? Maybe one day you'll close your eyes and wake up on the other side."

"With your mom?"

"Yes."

"I'd like that," he says, resting his head against my arm. "And one day you'll be there too?"

"Yes," I say. "And everyone who loves you. We'll all come and join you."

"I'll make it nice for you all." Tom's voice is like a wisp of dust, drifting up to me.

"You're not going anywhere for a long time, Tom," I say.

I wrap my arms tight around him and push my feet onto the ground, so we can swing together to the clouds.

. . .

"Left or right?" Blister holds his hands out to me. I tap the right hand and he uncurls it. The stone sits snug in the palm of his hand.

"Left it is, then." He's trying to pretend that nothing has changed, that my hair is all right and I'm still me.

I feel lost.

"Ready?" Blister asks. I nod and we bike off together.

The air feels blurry around us and it's hard work going

against the wind. It's warm, though. There's that feeling that the sky is trapping us in, that it's waiting to storm on us but it won't tell us when.

It takes longer than usual to get to the first crossroads. Blister bends down and picks up a white stone and passes it to me. I go to take it from him, but he pulls his hand away. And he kisses me. It's a kiss filled with something I can't name. The road has gone, the fields have gone, our bikes have gone. Just us.

My hair is short, but Blister still wants to kiss me.

He pulls away and gives me the biggest smile.

"You're still beautiful," he says.

And I want to shout to the horizon. Because Blister still loves me. Kathleen tried to break me, she tried so hard, but she didn't manage it. She couldn't. And she never will.

Blister passes me the stone. I hide it in one of my palms.

"Left or right?" I ask.

"Straight ahead."

"That's a field," I show him.

"We'd better go in it, then."

"It's against the rules."

Blister takes the stone from my hand. It leaves a chalky mark on my skin. He throws it far into the distance.

"We make the rules," he says.

I follow him as he wheels his bike through the knee-high grass. I try not to trample on the flowers, but it's difficult. When we lay our bikes down, we do it as softly as we can.

We push the stalks aside, so we can sit down together. If anyone drives by, they'll be able to see the tops of our heads peeking over the grass.

"I wonder how many miles we can see," Blister says.

"Ten?"

"More, I think."

"I'd like to touch the edge," I say.

"What do you think it feels like?"

"I think it's jelly-like."

"I think your hand would sort of disappear," Blister says.

"Into another world?"

"Maybe."

"I'd like another world."

"What if I'm not in it, though?"

"Then I'll stay in this world," I tell him. And I mean it. I'd live all the bad bits, just to have the good bits with him.

Blister leans over and kisses me again. A fire begins to burn just underneath my skin when he touches me. His hand on the back of my neck makes the field around us dissolve into nothing but Blister.

As he kisses me, his fingers touch my head. Under his palms, my ripped hair starts to heal. Somewhere, bit by bit, Blister begins to put me together again.

The noise makes us stop. It's a low rumbling in the distance, in the air and somehow in the ground too. We see it as soon as we look. Far away, a muddy corkscrew tumbles from the sky and drills into the ground.

"A tornado," Blister says. It moves quickly, kicking up the roads and fields underneath it, mesmerizing us. It's like a strange tower, beating its way across the land. There's something about it that's beautiful. I want to go to it and have it twist me up in its chaos, just to see.

"I don't know what to do," Blister says. I was so caught up in the dusty tower that I didn't realize how terrified he is.

"It's not coming toward us," I say, but he looks panicked.

"It'll change direction. They always do," he says.

"It's OK," I say. "But if it makes you feel safer, we can go back a bit." I stand up calmly, take his hand and we start to walk away.

The tornado is getting louder. I don't look back, but I've got a feeling that it's turning. That it's suddenly got us in its sights.

"Come on," I say. We start walking more quickly, with Blister glancing behind us.

"It's getting closer," he says.

"We're fine."

I look back. Blister is right. The tornado is thundering toward us, tunneling into the ground.

Blister pulls my arm and we start to run. The noise behind us is crashing closer, blocking out the thud of my heart. We're heading for a cluster of trees.

"Will they protect us?" Blister shouts.

"I don't know," I yell back.

The wind is hard against my back as we trample through the long stems of bitterweeds. We get to the first tree, both of us searching for breath. I know Blister wants to go further, but I need to turn and see it.

The tornado is roaring across the land. I've never seen one this close. It reaches down from sky to earth, its power and sound like nothing I've ever imagined. It smashes through the field, scooping up chunks of grass.

And it's trying to find us, to hunt us out.

Blister's face is streaked with fear. I want to tell him that it'll be OK, but I don't know if it will. I don't know whether it's safer to stay here, with some protection from the trees, or to try to sprint away. Could we outrun it?

I see the wheel first. The wheel of Blister's bike. Then mine. Both of our bicycles plucked from the ground and taken into the spinning cloud.

"No," I whisper. Without thinking, I start to run toward it. Blister pulls me back just as our shattered bikes are spat out by the tornado and fly tumbling to the ground. "No."

The tornado seems satisfied. It juts in a different direction again, running away from us.

"It might come back," Blister whispers, as though it can hear us. He has both his arms tight around me and we watch the tornado stalk off toward the horizon.

Quiet creeps in to take its place.

"Our bikes," I say.

"They're just bikes, June. We're safe," he says. We stand still together. Blister is shaking. "We could have died."

I move away from him and start to walk to where my bike fell. I don't want to see it.

But I find its wheel ripped from its body. A few feet away lies its twisted frame.

Blister is across from me, holding up his buckled bike. He examines it, as though it's something rare and precious. He looks out toward where the tornado was. The air is so still that it's hard to believe it was here.

I sit down next to my bike and hold the tattered wheel up to it. I know it's useless. I know it's gone.

Blister kneels down next to me.

"It could've been us," he says.

Part of me wishes it had been. That I'd stood in front of it, faced it head on and waited with open arms. It would have ripped my roots as it picked me up and thrashed my head in its swirling brown smoke. It would've taken me and made me free.

"Maybe Dad could fix it?" Blister holds up the skeleton of my bicycle. I just shake my head, because he already knows.

And he knows that, without my bike, I'm trapped. His house, our trailers, are too far for me to walk to. My bike meant me and Blister. It was Blister and me.

"We'll figure something out," he says, as though he can read my mind.

But if he really could, he'd see so much more. He'd see an anger building from a speck on the horizon, gathering everything bad in my life. Ripping it all up and binding it in an ear-splitting thundercloud. If Blister could see any of it, I don't think he'd love me anymore. I don't think he'd even want to know me.

• • •

We leave our broken bikes nestled in the grass. Blister says his dad will come with the trailer and pick them up. I don't tell him that I'd prefer to leave them here, lying twisted together on the earth.

It's calm now. The road we walk on is the same as when we left it. Through the fields, there's a zigzag of devastation where the storm walked, but nothing else is touched.

We hold hands tight.

"I thought it was going to get us." Blister sounds excited now. "I've never been so close. Tom will be so jealous. He wants to be a storm chaser when he grows up."

Little Tom, in the eye of the storm.

This is how the end could be. Together, we could stand in the twisting tunnel and it could take us away.

"I wonder where it is now," Blister says. "Does it just burn out?"

"I don't know."

"It must. It'll lose its strength and then turn to nothing."

The sky is clear now. It's cooler too, as though a lid has been lifted and the trapped air has found its way out.

"Blister?"

"Yes."

"I think Megan is Dad's real daughter." I just blurt it out.

He looks at me strangely. "What do you mean?"

"Kathleen said something. And the way she looked at me. She wanted me to know." We don't stop, but Blister's hand tightens around mine.

"You might have gotten it wrong," he says.

"No. I think it's true." The words feel too heavy to say.

For a moment there's nothing but the sound of our feet on the road.

"But you said Megan's dad was someone she'd never met."

"I thought he was."

"And she can't be your dad's daughter. Your mom died when you were six."

"I know."

"But Megan's only one year younger than you."

"Yes."

I wish I could hear Blister's thoughts.

"Do you really think so?" he asks.

I don't reply, but he knows what's in my mind.

"Oh, God."

I thought my dad had loved my mom. I thought they'd been happy. I thought that it had only been us three.

"What are you going to do?" Blister asks.

"I don't know."

"Will you ask him?"

"I don't know."

A truck drives past, kicking up the dust.

"But what if you find out that Kathleen was with your dad when your mom was alive? Would you really want to know?"

"Yes. I'd need to," I say strongly.

"But it'd be awful."

We still have so far to walk and already my shoes feel filled with sand.

"Do you think my mom knew?" I ask.

Blister breathes out heavily. "I don't know."

"I had no idea," I say.

"None at all?"

"No," I answer sharply.

I remember my mom and dad together, happy.

Blister takes his hand from mine and puts his arm over my shoulder.

"You can face whatever they tell you," he says. "I'll help you."

. . .

Blister's dad drops me half a mile from my house. He doesn't question why. Maybe he knows more than I think he does.

"Will you be all right?" he asks. I nod and he hauls the remains of my bike from the trailer. "I can tell your dad what happened, if you like."

"It's OK."

"Are you going to be able to get it home?"

"Yes. It's not too heavy."

"OK." He sweeps me into a hug. He smells of the Wicks' house and I want to hold onto him tight. "You just phone me if ever you want a lift to our house. I'm happy to come and pick you up."

"Thank you." I feel completely hollow.

I watch as he gets back into his car and slams the door. He leans out his open window.

"See you soon."

I think I'm going to cry in front of him, so I nod quickly and start to walk away. I hear his car go and leave me.

My bicycle is awkward to carry. I have to half drag it, but even that's difficult. I think about leaving it here and asking my dad to come and help me to get it, but I know I can't do that. I never want him to help me with anything again.

Megan is turning cartwheels on the front lawn. Kathleen is weeding the flower bed. Megan gasps as she sees me. Kathleen stands up straight and squints slightly in the sun.

It's hard to pull my bicycle through the gate, but I manage it.

"What have you done to your bike?" Megan comes up to me, but she doesn't get too close.

"It was a tornado."

"A tornado?" Kathleen almost spits.

"Dad's going to kill you," Megan says.

"It wasn't my fault." I take my bike to the side of the house and lean it against the wall. It bends away from the bricks.

Megan tries to follow me as I go into the house.

"What are you going to tell him?" she asks. I shut the front door behind me, so I can't see or hear them.

I find my dad in the living room. He has the television pulled out and is doing something with the wires. I go and stand as close to him as I can get.

"June?" He looks up, surprised.

"Is Megan your real daughter?" I ask.

I watch as his face crumples. I see the lies he wants to tell me get folded away and the expression that's left is hopeless.

"What do you mean?" he asks.

"You know what I mean. Is it true?"

"June." He pulls himself up to sit on the edge of the armchair.

"Did Mom know?"

He puts his face into his hands as though he can rub the shame away.

"Did she know?" I'm starting to shout, and he's looking toward the door. He holds his hand out to me, as if I'd want to take it.

"No," he says. "Yes. She found out."

"Found out?"

"Yes."

"That Megan was yours?"

"No, not that. She found out about Kathleen."

"When?"

He rubs his fingers over his creased forehead, over and over.

"A few months before she died."

My world creeps in around me.

"But Megan was five by then," I say.

"Yes."

"So you must have known Kathleen all that time."

Dad nods slowly. "Yes."

"But Mom loved you."

"It's complicated," Dad tries.

Kathleen's antique clock is on the mantelpiece. I run over and pick it up. Dad just has time to cover his head before I throw it hard at him.

On the wall, there's a picture of Dad and Kathleen on their wedding day. They smile out at me and I hate them. I rip it from its hook and hurl it at the wall. It smashes and the splinters pierce their perfect faces.

Dad jumps up and he tries to hold me, but I kick out at him. I break free and grab Kathleen's shepherd ornament from the shelf. I throw it at the wall and hear the china smash.

Kathleen and Megan come running in. They stop in the doorway.

I run toward them, but Dad pulls me back.

"Did you know?" I yell at Megan.

"Know what?" She moves a bit behind Kathleen as I shove myself out of Dad's arms.

"That he's your real dad!" I shout it so hard that my throat burns.

Megan stares at me. "Who?"

"Him." I point toward the dad I used to know.

The expression on her face changes. She looks lost.

"He's not," she says. She seems five years old again.

"Ask him!" I shout.

"I'm sorry." Dad tries to reach out for Megan, just as I look at Kathleen.

"I hate you!" I scream at her. Dad grabs me back again. *"I hate you I hate you I hate you!"*

Kathleen moves slowly behind the sofa, but Megan stands still, as though the words still don't make sense for her.

I kick Dad hard and he doubles over and I run from him.

I have nowhere to go. Without my bike, I'm trapped. I storm up the stairs and slam my door. I wedge my chair under the handle. I kick my bed again and again, before falling onto it and screaming into my pillow, hitting and hitting it. The anger is like a knot in me and it feels like it's growing. Its tendrils creep into my lungs, into my stomach and into my heart.

I scream until my throat is so sore that it burns to breathe.

I curl up into a ball. I want to disappear.

• • •

I won't eat breakfast with them. I'm silent as I pack my bag with bread and fruit. I take a bottle of water from the fridge.

"I want you to drive me," I tell my dad. I won't look at him. I'll never look at him again.

"Where?" he asks. He sounds defeated.

"Out."

"June, he's eating breakfast," Kathleen says.

"It's OK." Dad pushes his plate away and stands up. I go outside and wait for him by the garage.

I direct him where to drive. I'll get close to our trailers, but far enough away for him to never guess.

"I'm sorry," he attempts. I look away and try to block him out. "It wasn't easy. None of it was."

Go away go away go away go away go away.

"When you're older, maybe you'll understand."

"Mom was older. Did she understand?"

He can't answer that.

"I hate you," I tell him. His fingers grip the steering wheel.

"I can understand that," he says.

"And Kathleen and Megan. I hate them too."

"Megan didn't know," he says quietly.

The anger is stretching out inside me again. I roll the window down and put my hand into the air. It hits into me and calms me.

"I don't want to live with you anymore," I say.

"June, I know it's really tough for you. Just give it time."

"Is that what you said to my mom?"

I move my fingers in the wind.

He stops the car where I tell him. I get out, pull my bag over my shoulder and walk away. I don't even bother to close the door.

He doesn't start the engine. He must be watching me. I hold my head high and start to cut across a field, where there's no way he can follow. I walk on and eventually I hear the sound of his car. He must be turning it around on the narrow road and heading off back to his family.

．．．

Our trailers look worn this morning. They need a wash, but Blister and I rarely do it because it's difficult to get enough water up here.

I stop outside our kitchen. I lick my finger and draw a heart, just under its window. In the middle of it, I write our initials: mine and Blister's.

I bend down and wipe my finger on the grass.

Inside, a new paper shape hangs above the sink. I'm not sure what it's meant to be. It's gray, with strange coils coming off it.

The plate I get from the cupboard isn't very clean, but I use it anyway. I put my apple and the slices of bread on it. And I sit alone and eat.

I could live here. Blister could bring me water and I could shower at his house. It'd be too difficult to get to school, so I'd just never go back.

The bread is dry, so I open the bottle and drink some of the cold water.

I leave my bag on the table and go to our school room. Blister's books are stacked neatly on the floor. The top one has pieces of paper sticking out of it. When I pick it up, I'm careful not to let them drop out.

In his notebook underneath, he's drawn pages and pages of labeled diagrams. His handwriting looks like broken spiders' legs. It doesn't seem right for him.

Another book is about anatomy. On the front, a heart has been cut open. There are the veins where the blood flows in and out. There are layers of muscles that help it beat. There's a heart just like it inside me now. I put my hand on my chest and feel it faintly. If you cut through, you'd be able to see the different parts that make it work.

I hear someone jumping over our gate and landing with a thud on our side. I duck down, so they won't see me through the window. There are footsteps, but I'm not sure which way they're walking.

The door opens, and when Blister sees me crouching here he jumps back, startled. He nearly falls off the step and I laugh.

"June?" He sounds confused.

"Good morning," I say lightly.

"How did you get here?"

"Dad drove me."

It's back again. Everything my dad did with Kathleen is filling the trailer. I push with all my might to keep it away.

"He drove you here?"

"No. He dropped me off and I walked the rest."

Blister leaves the door open as he comes over to me. His kiss is warm and it loses me, just for a moment.

"Did you ask him? About Megan?"

"Yes." My voice is flat. "I was right."

Blister shakes his head. "I'm sorry."

"They didn't even bother to tell Megan."

"That's a lot for her to take in too," he says.

"I want to bury them all and dig them up when they're only bones," I say. Blister doesn't laugh.

"I'm not surprised," he says.

"We could paint their bones black and hang them from a tree," I say. Blister looks at me.

"I don't think that'd be such a great idea."

"You're the boss." I want to smile, but it's not there.

"What did they say about your bike?" he asks. I shrug. "Dad says mine is beyond repair," he says. "It's totally mangled."

"I don't want to ever go back, Blister."

"I bet you don't."

"Would your parents let me live at your house?" I ask.

He looks shocked. "Our house is fit to bursting, June."

"But I wouldn't even need a bed. I could sleep on the floor. And I could help your mom. I'd look after Tom."

"How would you get to school?"

"I could learn with you."

"My dad's struggling to teach us as it is."

"I could help him teach the little ones."

"You've got your exams soon."

"You don't want me to live with you," I say. The numb feeling I have inside me flares into pain.

"You know it's not that. But my parents already have seven kids. They can't take on anymore." He kisses the back of my hand. "Maybe you just need a few days for things to settle down. You might feel better about it in a while."

"Better?"

"I don't know." He shrugs awkwardly.

"You think that it'll all just disappear? That one day, it'll be OK that Megan is my dad's daughter?"

"That's not what I meant."

"Do you know what I think, Blister? Do you know what I've spent the whole night thinking?"

"What?"

"That my mom didn't drown by accident. I think she jumped in and got tangled in those reeds on purpose. I don't think she wanted to live."

Blister looks at me, but he doesn't say anything.

"Dad might as well have killed her," I tell him. "He hurt her so much that she jumped into that water and never wanted to come up again."

"You don't know that."

"I think it's true."

"She wouldn't have wanted to leave you, though."

His words slam into me.

If my mom had done that, then she knew she was leaving me. I wasn't enough to make her stay.

My chest is gripped tight.

I wasn't enough.

Even for my mom, I wasn't enough.

. . .

Mr. Wick drops me at the same point as yesterday. When he stops, I don't get out of the car.

"Can't I stay with you?" I ask. He raises his eyebrows at me and his warm eyes go wide.

"I don't think your dad would be too happy with that."

"I'd be happy, though."

"But you have a home. It's where you should be."

"I don't want to be there."

"What's up, June? Why are things so bad?"

"They just are."

"Do you want to talk about it?"

I look up at Mr. Wick and I wonder if I could. I wonder if I could risk him changing who he thinks I am. Would he understand? Would he think it was all my fault?

"No." Slowly I twist the strap of my bag around my fingers.

"Some things in life can seem really tough," Mr. Wick says. "There are things that seem like a mountain and you can't find a way around it, yet you don't have the energy to go over it, either. You always find a way, though, eventually. Us humans are very strong underneath it all."

I open the car door.

"Thank you," I say. I look at him and I know there's genuine concern in his eyes. But I've finally asked for his help and he said no.

I close the car door and walk away. I don't take my compass necklace off. I tuck it under my T-shirt, but I keep it on.

The air is colder. The weather is changing. Soon, I'll have to take my coat when I go to our trailers. I rub my arms to warm them, but it doesn't really work.

. . .

My bedroom door is closed. I know that no one is hiding in there as I can hear Dad, Kathleen and Megan downstairs in the living room.

I go in. It looks like confetti has been scattered all over my floor. My bottom drawer is open. My clothes have been thrown out. Next to them is my box of precious things. It's empty. Someone has cut my special things into tiny pieces. Blister's castle, my arrowhead flower, my mom's scarf. My tulip. The angel that Blister made me is littered like snow on my carpet.

I stare at it, unable to move.

My most precious things have been cut into pieces so small that I'll never be able to put them back together again.

I pick up Tom's ring. It's been stamped on so hard that I can't even fit it on my finger. The green heart is cracked.

I get the chair and push it up against the door. I pick up my pillow, and as I lie down among the remains from my precious box, I pull my duvet from my bed and hold it tight around me.

I ignore Dad's knocking on the door.

I ignore Kathleen calling me through the painted wood.

And I try to float far away, up to the clouds, where no one can hurt me.

Thoughts twist away from me and my head hurts. My hip aches, so I turn onto the other side. I keep my eyes shut tight. I don't want to see what they've done, to remember that someone has been in here and sliced my things to shreds.

My eyes open. It's night, but my heart is beating so fast. I was in a dream, but I can't find where I was. I know I was crying, but my mind reaches out to find the fragments and it disintegrates at my fingertips.

The room is quiet. The house is cold. Like a solid block of ice that I can't melt, however hard I try.

I push the blanket to the side and get up. It's silent as I walk down the stairs. The paint on the wall seems clammy under my hand.

In the kitchen, I click on the small lamp and open the fridge. I don't want the bread and milk that's waiting. Or the slices of ham, sitting on a plate, squashed under the plastic wrap.

I close the fridge and on its door, just where my fingers

hold the handle, there are the pictures that Megan drew when she was younger, pictures that would have taken hours.

The scissors are in the drawer and I pick them up quickly and cut through Megan's precious work. Through her crayon lines and inky trees. Through hearts, where her fingers have held the pen and made the shape over and over. I cut them all up into little pieces.

There's a photograph of Kathleen and Megan, held tight to the fridge door by a magnet of a cherry cake. I cut that picture too and pick up all the shreds and carry them into the living room, where I drop them on the wooden table near the window.

The carpet under my feet keeps me silent, as I go to the corner shelf and pick up the photograph of Dad and Kathleen last summer. I take the thin wooden frame and bend it until it snaps and I spread its splinters on top of all the cut-up memories.

In the small drawer, by the empty fireplace, are the matches. I take them out and strike one, looking briefly at the clever yellow flame, until I drop it onto pictures that I never want to remember, that I wish had never existed. They curl slowly at the edges. Kathleen's face twists and melts and lights the room with its glow.

But the flame has gone, leaving behind drips of charred paper, with half-formed pictures of Kathleen staring at me, telling me that I couldn't even get this right.

I go into the kitchen and take every proud piece of paper framed carefully on walls and tacked to cupboard doors. I open drawers and empty them of Kathleen's neat pile of household bills. In the hall, silently, I find her favorite scarf, waiting on its hook. I hate its smell and I cut it with the sharp scissors, ripping through the material. In the living room, I scatter it all among the ash on the wooden table.

I want to get rid of it. I want Kathleen to come down in the morning and I'll watch her face as she sees the charred remains of the things she loves and she'll know I've beaten her again. That every day I'm getting stronger and I'm slowly moving further out of her reach.

I strike a match and drop it onto the horrid little pile. I'd like to stay and see the flames flicker, but I know there's more that I want to add, before it goes out again.

I run silently to the cupboard under the stairs, where Kathleen keeps her precious things. I turn on the dim light and open the box where the photographs are kept. Row upon neat row of Kathleen and Megan smiling. I look through them, even though I don't want to. I want to forget their cruel faces. I search deep down to the bottom, to try to find one of my mom, but she's not here. I can't find one picture of her, tucked under the weight of all the others.

In the box next to it, I find some old schoolwork of Megan's. I sift through it all. On a little scrap of paper, there's a badly drawn apple and Megan's name looking hesitant and shaky. "Six years old," Kathleen has written in the corner.

Megan came here when she was six years old. My mother had drowned and here was a sister to make things better.

There's a smell of smoke. I grab clutches of these pieces of paper and run back toward the living room.

The sofa, the carpets, the curtains are on fire. It's all on fire. Black smoke curdles up across the ceiling.

I stare at the flames, so loud and angry that they'll wake Kathleen.

And I know she'll kill me.

I've burned her things. Her sofa, her chair. The curtains she spent so long choosing.

I run into the kitchen and fill a bowl with water, until the wet spills over the side. Across the hallway, the flames are bigger. It's too hot to get close. The water falls onto them and does nothing.

The smoke is hurting me. It looks thick and solid. The fire is roaring and it's covering my thoughts. There's so much of it.

"Dad!" I call up the stairs. But I'm not loud enough—I know I'm not. I'm terrified that it'll be Kathleen I'll wake and she'll throw me into the fire.

I know I have to get help. I try to go into the sitting room, to reach the phone, but my skin is boiling and the smoke is making me retch.

In the kitchen, I pull out drawers, trying to find Kathleen's phone, or Dad's. Any phone, just to get help. My eyes feel scratched as I yank at the cupboards, but there's nothing.

I have to wake them.

The flames are on the stairs. My nightgown is on fire. I stamp it with my hands.

I have to get to Blister.

Blister will know what to do.

I unlock the front door and open it. I start to run.

Behind me, the house explodes into a ball of flames.

AFTER

I remember only this.

. . .

They found me down by the river. I was alone, smelling of smoke.

They told me that I had killed my dad and I had killed Kathleen. That Megan might die. She had jumped from her window, but she was too high up and already caught by flames. They said I had lit a fire and run away and left them there to die. I didn't know what they meant. I had just wanted to burn the little things.

They took my hands and locked me up in a tiny room.

They said that I'd known the window keys were hard to reach. That maybe I'd even hidden them.

I cried that I didn't, but they wouldn't listen, that my dad was dead and I didn't know why and I wanted to die too.

Vomiting, day and night.

They drove me in a van and strangers banged hard on the side.

I wore a suit that wasn't mine, because all my other clothes were ruined.

The room was too big and I felt too small.

Fear raced through me so fast that it was difficult to stand up.

I didn't understand what the judge said. He used words I've never heard.

Blister was there, but I couldn't look at him, because I thought my heart would stop.

A lawyer sat with me. I said his name over and over in my head, to take away the other thoughts. *Mr. Johnson, Mr. Johnson, Mr. Johnson, Mr. Johnson*, until my head hurt too much and the smell of smoke seeped in again.

Two lines of men and women stared at me. The room was filled with words, about how I overturned tables and hit other children. How I didn't have many friends.

My teacher told them that she never saw any sign of Kathleen hurting me, that I never mentioned a thing. Kathleen always seemed concerned and loving.

They thought I wanted to kill them all.

And I heard Blister shout out. I turned and saw Mr. Wick whisper something in his ear. But my Blister shook his head and started to cry.

The judge said something, but my body was shaking. Pain seared through my belly.

I'd never seen Blister cry before. His shoulders jolted up and down. I remember how he wiped his eyes beneath his glasses with the backs of his hands.

The judge said something else. The lawyer patted my arm and turned me to the front.

And all I could hear was Blister weeping.

AFTER
five weeks later

The room is full. The judge is sitting at the front. He looks at me with a face so blank that I don't know what's inside his mind. He's talking about my dad, but it hurts so much that I have to close my thoughts and take myself away to another place.

There are no windows and I'm finding it hard to breathe.

Mr. Johnson puts his hand on my arm. He needs me to listen.

"June Kingston," I hear the judge say, "this court has prepared a comprehensive sentencing order, which is on file with the clerk." I watch his mouth move underneath his mustache. He continues speaking. There is the word *fire*, but it spins out of my reach and holds the other words tight with it.

I feel Mr. Johnson tense beside me.

"Therefore, June Kingston, as to count one, you are judged guilty of the crime of attempted murder. For this crime, the court sentences you to life in prison, with no possibility of parole."

"She's just sixteen!" Mrs. Wick screams out into the room. I turn to her. She's standing up, her arms thrown wide, as she looks toward the jury.

"As to count two, you are judged guilty of the crime of first-degree murder. For this crime, the court sentences you to be put to death in the manner described by law."

Everything stops.

My heart stops beating.

The world stops spinning.

I look to Mr. Johnson, because I can't have heard the words that have just been said. He's staring at the front, his hand tight on my arm.

"As to count three, you are judged guilty of the crime of first-degree murder. For this crime, the court sentences you to be put to death in the manner described by law."

They want me to die.

"*No!*" Mrs. Wick is crying. But she can't reach me.

The judge is speaking. Mr. Johnson is trying to talk to me.

"June Kingston," the judge says, "you are hereby remanded, and without bail, to the custody of the sheriffs of the Coryell County, to be delivered to the commitment of the Department of Corrections, where you will be confined until final executions of this judgment and sentence prescribed by law." He looks toward the jury. "This court is now in recess."

Blister's head is bent forward. His hands are shaking. He moves his thumbs around each other in endless circles, then he looks up at me.

They are helping me to stand, one on either side. My hands are clamped tight in the handcuffs. The noise of dragging metal follows me as I start to walk.

I think I might pass out, but they hold me up. I crane my

neck to look at Blister. He's standing up, his whole body shaking with tears.

"She's just a child!" I hear Mrs. Wick cry.

We're near the door. They're taking me away. I look to the jury. Some of them are crying. Some of them have faces of stone.

"Please," I whisper to them. "I didn't mean to."

The guard starts to open the door.

"June!" Blister yells, his voice cracking through the pain in my skull and reaching into my bones. "June!"

My legs give way. I try to stand, but they have to drag me out.

. . .

I can't see from the van. There are no windows and I'm in a cage. I want just a glimpse of the houses we pass. I want to see them change into flat fields. I want to see the trees and the sky.

I stare at the grille and count the lines. How many squares make up the whole?

But my dad comes through. His hands are blackened. I can't look at his face.

I didn't mean to do it, I tell him.

Kathleen is on the other side too. She's pushing up against the metal, trying to get to me.

I put up my hands to block her way, but she squeezes the smell of her burning bones through the squares. It's on my skin and every time I breathe I swallow it. Her death is inside me now.

Count to ten, Blister tells me. I close my eyes and imagine him here. He's holding my hand and wiping the tears from my face. *I'll make you a paper rope to help you escape.*

And I cling to him.

. . .

The van stops. I wait for it to move again, but it doesn't. It's loud as the back door is unlocked and daylight knocks into me. I close my eyes, but only briefly. I can't miss any of these last few minutes before they take me inside.

A woman unlocks the cage.

The monster gets out.

I step onto the ground and they start to move me.

"Wait," I say. The men keep walking, leading me by my elbow. "Please. I just want to touch the earth."

They look at each other and one loosens his grip. I bend down and place my bound hands on the ground. It is hard, covered with a layer of dust. It's the color of white sand.

I don't think I can stand up and they have to pull me straight. No one speaks to me as we walk. I keep the earth's dust on my palms.

. . .

This is more than terror.

They lead me through doors and gates with thick metal bars.

They put me in another cage and I have to take off my clothes. They watch me, naked, my flesh on show. My belly, my legs, my breasts, they see it all. There's no corner for me to hide in and humiliation ripples over my bare skin.

They check my mouth. Under my tongue. In my ears. I'm prodded and squeezed.

I am given a paper dress. So that I can't hang myself.

My body walks, but I'm not here. I'm racing fast in the blue air to reach Blister. I find him by a crossroads, waiting with a stone in his hand.

Left or right? he asks, putting his arms behind his back.

Left, I say, touching his hand. He unfurls his fingers and the stone is in his palm.

Left it is. He takes my hand and we start to walk.

The door is white, with bars sunk into the top half of it. They open it, then someone takes off the shackles around my ankles. I'm put inside the room. It's no more than a box.

"This is it," one of the men says.

It's too small. They can't leave me here.

But they do. They shut the door hard behind me. A slot in the door opens.

"Put your arms through."

I do as they tell me. Through the bars, I see the man move the key to unlock the handcuffs. I bring my arms back through. The flap closes. It's such a normal sound, just metal on metal, but it leaves me totally alone.

I stand staring out through the bars in the door. I don't want to look at the cell. I'm scared that it might build a fear in me that will make me go mad.

The floor of the corridor outside is shiny gray. The striplight reflects off it. Opposite, there is a white wall. I reach my arms out as far as they will go. It feels like dead air. I turn my palms upward toward the light.

I want to see my dad. I want to see my dad so much. I want him to wake me up.

There's a noise behind me. I turn, frightened. There's no one here. I pull my arms in. There's not even anywhere for someone to hide.

But there's definitely a whisper, hissing into the cell.

There's a square vent on the wall above the slab of bed. I have to stand on the thin mattress to reach it.

"Hey, new girl." There's a faint voice. "You there?"

I touch the grille with my fingers.

"New girl. You there?"

I look back toward the bars in my door. I'm scared to speak and I'm scared to stay silent.

"New girl?" The voice travels from another cell to mine.

"Yes," I whisper.

"Are you there?"

"Yes," I say louder. The voice chuckles.

"My name's Mickey," she says. "How you doin'?" It's difficult to hear. I have to push my ear right up close to the vent. "Not good, eh? Poor lamb. How old are you?"

"Sixteen."

An exhale floats down the vent.

"That's too young."

My legs can't keep me standing. I kneel on my bed, my hands flat on the thin blanket. My lungs aren't working. I reach out with my fingers, as if to grab the air, but there's none there.

"It's OK, girl," the voice says, somewhere in the distance.

The bars in the door blur into each other.

My breaths are too small. It's not enough.

"You'll get used to it." And her faint laugh wheezes into the room, until I have to cover my ears and wait to disappear.

. . .

I open my eyes. The room feels wrong. It's too dark and the bed feels the wrong way around. I sit up in a panic. And then I remember.

Dad. Dad. Dad.

My heart is beating too fast. I'm in a cell and they never want me to get out.

The blanket is thin around my knees. The wall is cool behind my back and I try to make it calm me. Blister is telling me to count to ten. I want to, but my dad is pushing into my mind. We're on our bicycles, laughing into the wind. He's reading me a story. He's throwing me high into the lake.

He was alive and I took it from him.

The wings beat in me. They fill me up and cram my throat.

They found him by the window. He almost escaped.

I can't breathe. I go to the bars in the door, but the air is stale. And the wings have left no space in my lungs.

I want to tell my dad I'm sorry. That I didn't mean for him to die. That I want him to come back.

I've never known fear like this. I'm a spider in the corner and they're going to crush me. All I can do is wait.

• • •

It's Thursday. Four days since I arrived here. They say that Blister is coming to visit.

I have mosquito bites on my arms and face. I've scratched them raw and he'll see them. My hair hasn't grown enough. He'll see that too.

I won't be able to touch him. Not once. I won't be allowed to feel his hand in mine.

But I'll see him. He'll be here.

• • •

They handcuff me through the slit in the door. They walk me down the shining corridor. I couldn't eat my breakfast and my stomach hurts. The light is making me dizzy.

The keys are loud as they lock and unlock.

I'm in a room divided into cages. In front of one stands an older woman. She smiles as she leans toward me.

"I'm Mickey," she says. Mickey from the vent. Mickey who's kept me alive these last four days. "My son and granddaughter are coming to see me." She beams.

I'm shaking. My palms are sweating. I wanted to look nice, for Blister.

"You'll be OK," Mickey says, and she reaches over and squeezes my hand. The guard steps forward and moves me away into one of the cages. He points to the telephone handset hooked onto the wall.

"When your visitor comes, speak into that."

Then he leaves, locking me in.

I sit down and look through the glass in front of me. It shows an empty room. The door on the back wall is closed. I stare at it.

Too many minutes pass. My chest feels clamped tight.

The door in the other room opens. A man comes in with a baby on his hip. Behind him, Mr. Wick walks through and with him is Blister. I start to cry. I don't mean to, I didn't want to.

Blister is crying so hard. He's trying to look at me, but he can't. His dad helps him to sit down on one of the chairs on their side, divided from other visitors by wire mesh.

Mr. Wick picks up their handset and I pick up the one on my side. It's cold and heavy in my hand.

"How are you?" His words get caught and he coughs slightly. "Blister's mom sends her love."

The thought of her standing in her kitchen makes my lungs burn. I want to be with her. I want to listen to her voice and hear Eddie yelling from the hall.

"I didn't mean to," I whisper.

"We know you didn't," Mr. Wick says. And I know he's trying not to cry.

Blister holds up his hand to the glass. On my side, I hold up mine. He's so close to me, but I can't feel his skin.

"I'm sorry," I tell him. He nods, biting his lips.

"So am I," he mouths, before the tears take him over.

Blister, it's you. You're here.

"How is the food?" Mr. Wick asks. I nod to him. "Do you share a room?"

"No," I say quietly.

"Maybe it's nicer on your own," he says.

No. I'm lonely. They hardly let me out. I'll go crazy.

"How is Megan?" I ask, and the air turns colder.

"She's still in a coma," Mr. Wick says.

"Will she wake up?"

"They don't know." His words wind down the wire toward me and end in silence.

"Can I speak to Blister?" I ask quietly.

"Of course."

Mr. Wick puts his hand on Blister's back as he passes him the handset.

I look into Blister's eyes. The pain in my chest stabs so hard that it's difficult to see.

"Can we bring you books?" Blister eventually asks.

"I don't know," I say.

"We'll ask," I think Mr. Wick says.

"Which would you like?" Blister asks.

"Anything," I tell him. My hand still touches his through the glass.

"Are they treating you OK?"

"Yes."

Blister is looking so hard at me.

"Is there a window in your room?" he asks.

My mouth is dry. I need some water.

"A small one, at the top. It's too high to look out of, but I can see the sky."

"The sky's good," Blister says.

I want to ask how Tom is, but I know that I'll fall apart if I do.

"Mr. Johnson is organizing your appeal," Blister says. "He thinks that it might be as soon as three months."

"And then they'll let me go?"

Mr. Wick looks down at his hands, but Blister's eyes don't leave mine.

"I'll get you out," he says.

. . .

It's been maybe five days since I saw Blister. The days here are endless and blend into one.

The slot in my cell door opens and a book is pushed through. It's a paperback, but it feels heavy in my hands. I open it to look at the words. They're black, against the white pages, tidy in their rows. I breathe in the smell of the paper, the smell of the world outside.

Somewhere, out there, in a huge room with machines clunking and whirring, this book was put together. People touched it, their fingerprints smeared with living. I put my hand on the cover, but I can't tell who they are, where they are.

The writing on the back says that it's about a girl who can sing. I think that Blister sent it to me. He chose it for me.

I sit on the bed and open it. I read the first line. And then I read it again. And then I let myself go into the page, far away from here. I'm somewhere else and they'll never be able to find me.

AFTER

one week later

I'm led into a small room. Instantly I know the man is a priest.

"June?" he asks. "I'm Reverend Shaw."

I'm clamped in handcuffs, but still he wants to shake my hand.

"I'm pleased to meet you," he says.

I look to the warden at my side.

"You don't have to stay," he tells me blandly. But I'm outside of my cell, if only for a short time, and I'm grateful.

"I'm here to help you," the reverend says. I nod. "Do you want to sit down?" He gestures to the table. On top of it sits a small vase of flowers.

I don't answer him, but I shuffle forward and sit on the chair, pushed back against the wall.

"You can leave us," Reverend Shaw tells the warden. The man looks at me briefly, as though he doesn't trust me, before he steps outside the door.

"Some people like me to read to them," the reverend says, sitting down opposite me. His face has gentle lines.

"I didn't mean to do it," I say quietly.

"I'm not here to judge," he says.

"Do you believe me?"

"I believe in the power of forgiveness. The strength of love."

"My dad died because of me. How can I ever be forgiven?"

"You have to start by forgiving yourself." His words fall heavily around me.

"That's not possible."

"It is. It takes strength and courage and you have those, June."

"I'm so frightened," I whisper.

"I know." Reverend Shaw puts his hand lightly on top of mine. "But I'm with you," he says.

I put my head in my hands and weep.

• • •

I think that the mosquito bite on my cheek is infected, but they won't give me any cream. They say it'll clear up if I stop itching it. But I've tried and I can't stop. And now Blister is coming again and I look even worse. He'll never want to kiss me again.

The handcuffs are on and they lead me through all the doors. Two other prisoners stare as we walk past. One of them I've never spoken to. The other is Sarah-Jane. She's in the cell next to mine and I hear her pacing, all the time. Up and down, four steps one way, four steps back. I have to block my ears, or my anger would take over and then I'll never get out.

Blister is the first person into the visiting room. For a

split second, I'm happy and I think I can run to him. Then I remember that glass keeps us apart. My whole body jolts with the shock of it.

Mrs. Wick is walking behind him. Her head is held high, but she looks terrified.

They sit down and Blister picks up the handset, holding it close to both of them so that his mom can hear me too.

"Hey," Blister says. He puts his hand up and I put mine as close to his as it will go.

"Hey, you."

He's not crying, but he looks torn apart.

"June," Mrs. Wick mouths. "How are you?"

"I want to go home," I say.

She puts a transparent plastic bag onto the thin table in front of them. There are a few coins and some keys in it. Her car keys. I think of all the times that I've sat with them in their car, the windows rolled down, singing to the wind.

"Did you get my book?" Blister asks. Even his voice sounds different. It doesn't belong here.

"Yes. Thank you."

"I spent a long time choosing it," he says. "I didn't know what to get."

"It's perfect."

"We're allowed to give you some food from the machine," Blister says. "The officers will bring it through to you."

"Thank you."

Unease circles around us. When we had all the time in the world, we could talk about anything. But now we don't and I don't know what to say.

"Dad sends his love," Blister says. I nod. "Tom misses you." I nod again, over and over, to try to keep the tears away. "He

217

made Dad make him a double swing, so you can sit on it with him when you come out."

"How is he?" I manage.

"He's fine," Mrs. Wick says too quickly. I look from one to the other.

"Has he been sick?" I ask. I want to know the truth. I don't want any more lies.

"He's got another infection," Blister says. "But he's getting better."

"Tell him that I'm hugging him," I say. "And that I'll never stop."

Blister smiles, but not enough for his dimples to show.

"How's studying?" I ask.

Blister shrugs slightly. "It's difficult."

"You have to keep going, Blister," I tell him. "You're going to be a doctor and change the world, remember?"

"I'll try."

The sadness sitting on us is so heavy that nothing we say can lift it. With every word, I'm closer to them going.

"Is Megan awake yet?" I ask quietly. Blister shakes his head.

She's sleeping, with tubes drifting in and out of her.

"She will get better, won't she?" I ask, but neither of them replies.

I stare at the white wall and wish that I could rearrange Megan's life. I'd change it all, right from the beginning. I'd give her a different mom and a different dad.

"I'm going to leave you two alone for a bit," Mrs. Wick says. I want to hug her goodbye. I think she's crying because she turns away from me and walks quickly out of the room.

I look at Blister.

"Have you got another bike yet?" I ask.

"My mom's cousin has an old one I can have," he says. "And I'm saving up to buy you one."

"You'll buy me one?"

"Yes."

"What color will it be?" I close my eyes.

"What color would you like?"

"Purple," I say.

"Purple?"

"Yes." It's just Blister and me, sitting together in our trailer. Our palms are touching and soon he'll kiss me.

"I'll get you a purple bike," he says, but the choke in his words makes me look up.

He's been crying and I didn't know. His hand is on mine, so he can't wipe away his tears.

"You don't like the color." I try to laugh.

"I miss you so much, June."

"I miss you, Blister," I say, before the pain swoops in and takes us both away.

. . .

The envelope has been opened, but it's addressed to me. From inside it, I pull out a purple paper bicycle. It's out of proportion and the seat is tiny, but it's beautiful.

There's a note with it, in Blister's spidery handwriting:

They wouldn't let me use glue. X

I hold the bicycle up in front of me. Blister has folded each line so carefully. I want to unfold it and do it again, just so my hands can be exactly where his were. But I don't want to ruin it. I smell the paper, but I can't find his smell on it. I turn the bicycle over and over, imagining Blister's fingers on it.

I love it, I tell him.

He's put a single line of thread on it. The only place I can hang it from is the bars in my door. I loop the fragile thread around and tie a knot. My purple bicycle hangs down, flat against the shiny paint.

And my heart breaks into a million tiny pieces.

. . .

Mickey and I walk in the yard. The sky is white cold, reaching down to touch the walls high on every side of us.

"Where shall we go today?" Mickey asks, shuffling slowly beside me.

To Blister's and my trailers, I want to say, but I know it'll hurt too much to go there.

"We could go for a picnic?" Mickey suggests. "How about alongside that stream?"

I look hard at the bricks until they dissolve, and we're walking through the grass toward the water. I want so much to hear the sound of it sliding past, but the quiet of the wind is all there is.

"Are you OK, June?" Mickey asks. We don't stop walking; we won't let the grass disintegrate into the dust that's beneath our feet.

"I miss Blister."

"I bet he misses you too."

I didn't want to hear that. I wanted her to say that he's all right without me.

"He says my appeal might be in a few weeks," I tell her.

Mickey doesn't say anything for a while. I think she's listening to the stream.

"You can't depend on that, girl," she finally says. "Or you'll go crazy."

"But Blister says that they could let me go."

"Then, if that's what you want to hang onto, you hang onto it. We've all got different ways of coping. You do yours and I'll do mine."

"Why are you in here, Mickey? What did you do?"

There's an uneasy silence. I meant never to ask her. I don't think I want to know.

"If I tell you," she says at last, "you won't see me as human anymore."

"I won't ever think that, Mickey."

But she doesn't say another word.

AFTER

six weeks later

"I only live when you're here," I tell Blister. He looks gaunt and so tired.

"You shouldn't be in here," he says.

"Yes, I should."

"But you didn't mean to do it."

"I killed them, Blister." The words are distant to me. I have to pluck them from far away and put them in the right order.

Blister rubs his eyes. When he looks up again, the hurt has gone even deeper.

"A lot of people think you shouldn't be here," he says.

"They send me letters," I say quietly.

"They do? Saying what?"

"That they're signing petitions to try to get me out."

Blister looks brighter. "It'll work," he says. "If enough people sign, they'll have to listen."

"I fold their letters into flowers," I tell him. "I don't make very good ones."

Blister stares at me for the longest time.

"What's it like?" he asks so quietly.

"Lonely."

And he nods, as if he knows. But he can't. It's a loneliness I never knew existed. An impossible loneliness. A silence inside that strips away your soul.

"Maggie's got a new job," Blister suddenly says. "She's moving to Oklahoma City."

"But what about Jack?"

"She says she prefers the job to him."

"Oh. I thought she liked him."

"He was OK," Blister says.

I want to ask him how our trailers are, but I can't. And he never talks about them.

"Chubbers broke his bed by jumping on it. Dad's not happy."

"The one he made?"

"It took him every weekend for six weeks," he says flatly.

"Can he fix it?"

"Yes. It'll just take time."

I look at Blister and imagine his house, the chaotic rooms, the windows full of light. I could get lost there, but I know we haven't much time left.

"Mr. Johnson says Megan is much better. She's even walking around," I say.

"Can she help?" Blister asks. "At the retrial, can she say what Kathleen did to you?"

"How can she, when she did it to me too?"

"She won't get into trouble. She'll be telling the truth. And then they'd understand that you were just trying to burn their things. Megan could help get you free."

The door on Blister's side opens and the officer comes in.

Panic rushes into me, as it always does when visiting hours are over. I just want to be able to reach out and hold Blister's hand, to keep him with me, but I can't even touch him. Through the glass, I can see the fear in his eyes too.

"I'm OK," I try to tell him.

He doesn't move.

"I'll get you out," he says.

The other visitors are leaving and the officer is walking toward him.

"You have to go," I whisper.

He leans forward, his mouth to the glass. I try to kiss him, but he's pulled backwards.

He looks terrified.

I want to tell him that I love him, but the tears beat my words down.

And he's gone. The door is closed. The room where he was is empty. And they're helping me up and leading me away.

AFTER

four months later

"We'll try again," Blister says. He has a hardness about him, a determination that wasn't there before. "That's just the first appeal."

Mr. Wick takes the handset from him. "Mr. Johnson is already working on the next one," he says. He's grown a small beard and I wish I could reach out, just to feel what it's like. "It's OK, June—it's just a setback. And the petitions are still going strong."

"Are they?" I ask, my voice empty.

"*Yes!*" I see Blister shout. He slams his hand on the table. His dad leans over to touch his arm.

"People don't write to me so much anymore," I say. Yet I prefer it this way.

"Don't give up, June," Mr. Wick says. "Mr. Johnson thinks the next appeal will be up and running within a few weeks and it should be heard a few months after that."

"He told me that Megan's speech is getting better."

"That's good news." Mr. Wick nods his head.

"Do you think she'll testify?" I ask. They glance briefly at each other and I know their answer.

Blister takes the handset from his dad.

"I've decided something, June." His black eyes look alive. "I'm not going to be a doctor."

"No," I say. He can't mean it. He's spent so much time working for it. "You can't do that, Blister," I say.

"I can. I'm going to be a lawyer. I'm going to be the best lawyer this country has ever seen."

No. Don't change your dreams for me.

"But you're going to find cures. You're going to save lives."

"I will be saving lives. Just in a different way." He touches his fingers to mine, but I can't feel them. "I'll have a head start. I'm going to begin studying for it now, alongside the school-work I do with Dad."

"You'll be great," I say quietly.

"I've been thinking," he says to me. "Maybe you should study something too. You wanted to be a vet, once," he reminds me.

"When I was twelve."

Mr. Wick leans toward the phone. "What would you like to be now?" he asks.

Free.

"Maybe *you're* the doctor," Blister says eagerly. "All these years we thought it was me, when all along maybe it was you. You were good when we learned things together."

"You have to be really bright," I remind him.

"You *are* bright, June," Blister says. "You're easily good enough."

"How can I study to save lives, when I took two away?"

226

My words stun them. Sometimes, I think they forget what I've done. But I never do.

"That's different," Blister tries.

Mr. Wick doesn't say anything. He must find it hard to look at me, because he's staring intently at his hands as he traces his wedding ring with his thumb.

"I'd like to be a social worker," I say. Blister doesn't take his eyes from me.

"I never knew that," he says.

"Neither did I," I reply.

"You'll be the best social worker there is," he says, his face strong again.

"I will, won't I?" Despair winds its way in and out of my words.

"Yes, you will." Blister smiles, his dimples deep. "You will."

AFTER

eighteen years old

"June." Mickey's voice drifts through the vent. She takes me out of the paper world I'm in. "Are you there?" Her voice sounds bleak. "Course you're there. Where else would you be?"

I sit up, pull the blanket around me in the shallow dark and press my lips as close to the little grate as I can.

"Yes, I'm here," I say.

"Did I wake you up?"

"No. I wasn't sleeping," I say. There's silence. Nothing. "Mickey?"

"I miss my son, June," she finally says.

"I know." Her sadness sits heavy in my chest.

"And I miss Jade."

"You'll see them soon. Just two days and you'll see them again."

"I want to see them every day."

"I know you do."

"At home, my son lived just two doors from me. Did I tell you that?"

"Yes."

"I can picture Jade's room. Where her bed is. My son puts my pictures on her wall."

"Even the fish ones?" I laugh.

"Not the fish ones." I think I've made her smile. I hope I have. "But I want to tuck her in, June. I want to kneel by her bed and read her a story. I want to stroke her hair until she goes to sleep." The sadness in her voice is so deep now. "I'm going to miss her first day of school, every birthday, every Christmas."

"You might get out, Mickey."

"I don't deserve to." Her words fall into my room. The grille cuts them up and scatters them across my bed.

I put my hand on the wall to steady myself.

"We can't make it different, can we?" I whisper. It's too quiet for Mickey to hear.

"Tell me something good, June," she says.

Something good.

It's difficult for good things to find their way in here. These blank walls sometimes make me think that nothing else really exists.

"Aster flowers are good," I say. "Their purple color is something else."

"It is," Mickey says.

"We'll see some aster flowers on our walk tomorrow," I say. Mickey laughs so sadly. "We'll find the biggest field, filled with the biggest flowers, and we'll sit in it and stare at the beauty of the sky."

"Not the sky," Mickey says. "I'll look closely at the grass. I miss the insects, the bugs, all the animals."

"Did you know that ants never sleep?" I ask.

Mickey laughs gently. "Where did you learn that?"

"Blister," I say.

Blister Blister Blister.

I close my eyes to see the field more clearly. I reach out to touch the grass, to feel the green on my fingers.

"I was bitten by a snake once," I say. Mickey doesn't reply. "It was hurt and Blister and I wanted to save it. He picked it up and we made a nest for it in our trailer. But it bit me."

"Did it hurt?"

"Yes. But it got me into a hospital, where I nearly told the nurse about Kathleen. I tried so hard to tell her, but I couldn't." I lean my forehead against the wall. I'm so close to the grate that I can smell the dust and rust trapped in there. "I would look at the nurse and beg her to read my mind, you know?"

"Yes," Mickey says. "I know."

"My arm was swollen for weeks and every time I saw it I was so angry with myself. The snake bite got me to a safe place where I could tell and I didn't do it."

"What happened to the snake?"

"It died."

"That's a shame."

"Blister didn't even bury it. He was angry that it'd hurt me, so he just threw it in the bushes." I remember Blister's earnest eyes as he'd told me. But he was smiling so much, because I was back, after two weeks away.

I hear Mickey's worn breath fall heavily into the room. "I never told either, June," she says quietly.

• • •

230

"How many prisoners have you lost?" I ask Reverend Shaw.

"Too many." He hangs his head slightly, his eyes on the open Bible in his hands.

"Do you ever feel angry?"

"Often. But I read this." He holds up his Bible slightly. Its pages are worn from years of use. "And I talk."

"Talking doesn't bring dead people back."

"No, but it helps me to sort out my thoughts. Sometimes, there are too many of them—I have to let them go."

"But how do you cope with all the people you lose? In here, how do you say goodbye?"

Reverend Shaw knows what I'm asking. I've wanted to find the way to these words for so long and now they've fallen in front of us.

"It's very difficult," he says. I've never seen him awkward. "Sometimes, I question whether I can keep doing it."

"Is it very final?" I ask. He won't look away from me. "Death."

"I believe it's just the beginning."

"Will I see my mom there?" I ask.

"I believe you will."

"And my dad?" My voice begins to crack. "What if he doesn't forgive me?"

Reverend Shaw looks at me steadily. "I think he already has."

"But I took his life."

"You didn't mean to."

"He died because of me. If I hadn't hated Kathleen so much, I never would have lit the fire."

"Where does the circle start, though? You suffered terribly, June. And I've no doubt that Kathleen suffered in her life too."

"Kathleen?"

"No one is born bad, June."

"She was."

"She was a vulnerable child once, and I think someone probably hurt her too."

"No one could hurt her." Anger reaches up inside me. I remember my days and nights pieced together by terror.

"Maybe if you try to understand her, forgiveness will be easier."

"There's nothing to understand." I've never raised my voice to Reverend Shaw before.

"It's not easy."

"What do you know about it?" My yelling shocks him. "Did she torture you? Did she try to destroy every part of you?"

"She didn't succeed, though." He puts his hand gently on me, but I yank my arm away.

"Didn't she? Look at me. Look at my life. I've got nothing left."

"You have, June."

"But they want me to die. They think I'm not good enough to live." I'm finding it difficult to breathe.

"You are good enough," Reverend Shaw says. "And you are loved."   .

The door unlocks.

"We're fine," Reverend Shaw tells the warden.

"She needs to go back to her cell," the man says.

"She's allowed to be angry," Reverend Shaw replies, his voice rising.

"Not on my watch." The warden strides over toward us and pulls me up.

"No!" I cry, and try to thrash out with my legs.

"June." Reverend Shaw kneels next to me. He's trying to calm me.

"I want to stay with you," I beg.

But another officer comes in and they're dragging me out the door.

"Don't let Kathleen win," I hear Reverend Shaw say, but the rest of his words are crushed by the metal doors locking behind me.

AFTER

six months later

"How's your studying?"

"It's good," Blister replies. "At the moment, I'm doing Civil Procedure." He has so much energy, contained in the room. "Mr. Johnson says that the third appeal should be in three months."

"Three months?"

"Yes," Blister says. He doesn't know how every second stretches in here. "But, June, I'm not sure about him anymore."

"Why?" Mr. Johnson has been the line of hope I've been holding onto.

"I'm not sure he's good enough. I think he's made mistakes. And he hasn't tried hard enough to get Megan involved. With someone else, I'm sure we can win it."

"Blister, I don't have anyone else."

Blister glances quickly to the side.

Through the mesh wall next to him, I can just see Mickey's

granddaughter as she begins to cry. It hits me hard that this isn't a place for her. This isn't a place for anyone to be.

Blister looks back at me. He suddenly looks too vulnerable on the other side of the glass.

Mickey's son looks bewildered as he gathers up his daughter. He says something to his mom, before he takes his crying child from the room.

When it's quiet, Blister continues. "I'm trying to persuade Mr. Johnson to go over Mrs. Andrews' statement again. And I'm sure we can find something in your old school records."

"You can't make your whole life about this, Blister," I say.

There's a scream, so loud that I can hear it in my cage. I look through the bars behind me. They're dragging Mickey out. She's trying to kick at the door as she thumps her hands raw on the wall, her fists clenched tight.

Another officer comes in. Mickey lashes out at the two of them, until more arrive and she's screaming as they drag her away.

We can hear her, even through the thick, locked doors. Her screams getting quieter. Until they're not there.

As if she never was.

AFTER

nineteen years old

"You're not wearing your glasses," I say to Blister. He looks awkward, touching his face where they should be.

"I'm trying contact lenses."

"Why?"

"I wanted to see what they're like."

"I prefer your glasses," I say. He doesn't smile. "How's your mom?"

"Getting better. The doctors said it was a clean break, so it should be easy to heal."

"How long will she be in a cast?"

"Another two weeks."

"It must be difficult for your dad."

"Yeah. It's not been the easiest few weeks."

"And coming here can only make it harder for you," I say, not letting him take his eyes from mine.

"It's OK."

"I don't know if it is anymore," I say calmly, even though

my heart is beating so hard that it hurts.

"I won't stop coming to see you, June."

"But what if it's not what I want?"

"I'll still come." He tries to smile. "Did you get the book Mom sent you?"

I nod. "Blister, please, you have to listen."

He looks away from me, down at his hand. He doesn't want to hear the words that I don't want to say.

"I need you to live a life for both of us." I sound strong, even though I'm turning hollow inside. "I want you to use every day for something good."

"But coming here is good." He sounds so like the boy who saved me, the boy who took me from Kathleen and reminded me how to be happy.

"Nothing about here is good." My hands ache to hold his face close to mine, to make him look at me again. "I'm taking your freedom away too, Blister."

"I don't want it."

Anger suddenly boils in me. "Yes, you do. You can't save the world by staying tied to this prison."

"But what about your world?" he asks quietly as he looks up at me.

"You'll always be in it."

• • •

I rip a piece of paper carefully from my book and I fold it and fold it and open it up until the shape appears. I'm trying to make a swallow, with its thin body and elegant wings, but I can't remember how. I need Blister to help me.

Yesterday, I tried to make a dragonfly. I wanted to hang it

on my door. But it was impossible without Blister. Everything is impossible without Blister.

The strip of window is white today. These are the worst days. It just mingles with the wall and I can barely see where one begins and the other stops. The world outside is lost to me and I think it may have disappeared altogether. I watch for a clue that it still exists. A bird, or a splash of blue. It can be hours with nothing.

Hours to think about why I didn't just tell. Why I was so terrified that it stopped me from speaking. How Kathleen had my mouth trapped shut with fear.

The slot in the door opens. I get up and put my arms through. The handcuffs are on, so they open the door. It's the officer with the trousers stretched too tight across her legs. Maybe that's why she moves so stiffly.

She shackles my ankles. I shuffle forward, with the loud clink of metal shadowing my every move. It's good, though. Good to be out. To feel the floor beneath my feet. To see hints of the rest of the building, edges of corridors, closed doors. Windows. I love the windows.

We go through the internal double gates.

Through the door.

And the air is on my face. I tip my head back, as I always do, keep my eyes shut tight and breathe the deepest I can go. I want to fill my insides up with air, to have enough to keep me going.

As usual Mickey is already here, pacing around on her own, as close to the edge of the wall as possible. When she walks past, I join her.

"Shall we go to the woods over there?" Mickey asks.

I look to where she points. I try to see the woods, but today there's nothing there.

"I can't see beyond the walls," I say.

"Try harder, girl," Mickey says. But there are only bricks, stacked one on top of the other, blocking us in.

Slowly, our feet shuffle forward on the ground.

"I wish it'd rain," she says. Her voice is rubbed raw from her years of being in here.

"It will." I look up at the blank white. I like the feel of rain falling all the way down here. It makes me know that I'm part of something much bigger. When it rains, it moves from us, over the wall and across the fields. It will fall on a child a hundred miles from here.

But they won't know it fell on us first.

"Do you think it's wrong if I don't want to forgive?" I ask Mickey.

"They hurt you a lot," she replies. "It's a lot to forgive."

"It is. And it feels like, if I do, then what they did becomes all right. When it wasn't. None of it was all right."

"I think the first person that you should forgive is yourself. I see the guilt eating you up, June. It poisons you."

"I don't know how to," I say. The walls suddenly seem even higher around us, the sky just that bit further away.

Mickey nods. "Forgiveness takes a lot of courage."

"I don't know if I have that," I say.

Mickey stops walking and looks at me.

"June, you're one of the bravest people I know."

"Have you forgiven yourself?" I ask.

"I have to, June, because I'm running out of time."

"Don't say that, Mickey."

"My clock's almost stopped ticking," she rasps out. "But it's better for my son this way. It's ruined his life. He works his hours, his days, his weeks around visiting. He might as well be in here with me."

"He wants to see you, though."

"But it's not right." Mickey's voice scratches slightly. "You heard that saying? That if you love someone enough, then you've got to set them free? That's why I want this over with. I don't want to keep him in this prison anymore."

"I don't want you to go anywhere, Mickey."

She laughs sadly and struggles into rattling coughs.

"My son says he wants to be there. That he wants me to know that he's with me. That I'll think only of him, sitting on the other side of that glass."

It's a horror I don't want to imagine.

"What about you, June? Who'll be there for you?" Mickey asks.

"I won't let them kill me," I say.

"Your mom will be waiting on the other side, girl," she says. "Open arms for sure."

And it hits me like a bolt. Whips any words clean from me.

Because, soon, Mickey's voice will go and then mine will too. The sight of me, the sound of me, my heart, my hands, my skin, my bones. There'll be nothing left.

I look to the sky and beg for a miracle.

. . .

I push my face to the bars in my door and I can see Mickey, moving in shackles down the corridor, flanked by two guards. She's almost doubled over. She can barely walk.

"Mickey," I whisper. She's crying so hard that she doesn't even see me as she goes past. "Mickey," I say louder, but she doesn't look back. I thought she would be strong. I thought she'd be able to hold her head high. But the sound of her tears echoes and fills the place.

They almost drag her along. Two arms are around her back. She's the terrified little girl whom no one would help. She's crying and there's the key in the lock for the next corridor.

She's disappearing.

I press my ears to the bars, desperate to hear the last trace of her.

They are taking Mickey to the Death House. For one more day and one more night, she'll be alone in a strange cell. Maybe tomorrow morning she will wake and wash her face and brush her teeth. Her comb will get stuck slightly in the tangle of her night hair, but she will gently work it through and then clip her hair back from her face with the big, brown barrette that I've never seen her without.

I think she will struggle with her breakfast.

Maybe she'll write a letter to her son. And maybe one to Jade. And all the time her heart will be hammering to get out. Trying to get out before they stop it from beating.

They'll unlock her door and Mickey will be led to her final room. The gurney will be waiting, its leather straps ready to hold her thin arms. She won't cry, as they help her onto it.

"Thank you," she will say to the man who supports her.

Watching her through the glass will be her son. He's twenty-six years old. Mickey is leaving him, and the pain almost blinds her.

"I'm OK," she will say, nice and slow, so that he can hear her words.

Mickey will lie down without being told.

They will tie her into the straps, across her stomach and her chest, and they will pull the buckles in hard.

"Do you have anything you wish to say?" the man by her side will ask.

"I want them to know that I'm sorry," Mickey will say, her voice husky in the tense air.

And then they will drip the liquid in. And with every drip she will go further away.

Further and further, until she's gone.

• • •

"I wanted to see you last week," Blister says. "But they wouldn't let me."

"I wasn't allowed visitors." My voice sounds cold but I don't want it to.

"What did you do?" he asks, his voice coming through the coil toward me.

"I was angry and trashed my room," I say. He's looking down at where the phone connects to the wall. "They killed Mickey."

Blister winces as I say it, as though he's physically hurt.

"Her case was different than yours, June."

"She's not a case. She's a person."

"I know." He drops his head down and runs a hand through his hair. I haven't seen him cry for so long and I can't even hold him.

I can't do this to him anymore.

Breathe, girl, I'm with you.

"Blister, I don't want you to come here for a while."

"You can't stop me from coming to see you." His eyes meet mine and I can see hurt settled so deep in him.

"I can." I have to look down. I need to have the strength to say these words, and I know that if I look at him I won't be able to set him free. "I'll stay in my cell. I won't come here to you."

"They'll make you." His voice sounds desperate. I know he wants me to look at him.

"No, they won't."

"Why won't you see me?" The words crack apart and Blister barely whispers them.

"You know why," I say quietly. "It's what I want, Blister."

"Look at me, June," he says. And I have to. I have to see Blister's face, every line, every trace of him. "You really want me to stop coming here?" His forehead is creased with years of pain.

"Yes," I say, my eyes looking into his.

Slowly, he nods.

"And I need you to concentrate on your studies, to get me free," I smile. I want his life to keep moving, even though mine has stopped.

Blister rests his head on the telephone.

I look at his forehead, his eyes, his neck. I need to remember it all. His shoulders, his arms. The hands that held mine. His lips that kissed me.

I hold my hand up to the glass. Blister raises his hand and presses it against mine. I imagine that I can feel his skin.

We look at each other, our fingers touching.

"Don't cry," I whisper.

"I'm sorry."

But I'm crying too. He tips his forehead onto the glass and I do the same.

My Blister.

He moves his head back.

"I'm sorry," he says again, quietly.

"No. I want you to be free."

He takes his hand away from mine. Through the glass, I can see that he's shaking.

He looks at me, so carefully, at every part of my face.

"I love you, June," he says.

"I love you too, Blister."

He puts the phone handset back in its place. Slowly he pushes his chair back and gets up.

He turns away. It's a few steps across the room.

The officer opens the door for him. Blister is about to go through, when he looks back.

Through my tears, I see my beautiful Blister standing there. He's crying so much that he has to hold the wall to steady himself.

"June," I'm sure he says.

And he's gone.

AFTER

two days later

It's best not to think. It's best not to remember.

If I just look at the window of sky and watch it change, then the world can become only this and nothing can hurt.

When things from my past appear in my mind, I paint them with the gray of the walls. I take a brush and wipe them clean away, before they burrow deep and can't find a way out.

The vent is silent.

Maybe I'll pretend it never gave me any words.

I'll just wake. Eat. Stare at the wall, as I wait for the next meal. And the next. I'll taste each mouthful.

And maybe be happy when I walk outside on my own in the fragile air.

I'll do as they say. Go out when they tell me, get shut back up inside when they want.

I'll read.

And maybe fold a paper shape where Blister's hands have never been.

And I'll try really hard to forget.

. . .

"June," Reverend Shaw says, "don't give up hope."

He holds my hands in his.

"Have faith, June. I'm with you."

But I'm adrift and I can't find him.

"This is just another kind of death," I say.

"No. You're alive, June. And while you have breath you must keep fighting. You must have hope."

Hope.

The word has become too difficult to catch.

"It's gone."

AFTER

twenty-four years old

She is looking down at her lap when I walk into the visitor booth. Megan. Instantly, I'm a child again and flooded with fear. She must know that I'm here, on this side of the glass, because she looks up.

"June," she mouths to me.

I don't want to sit down.

She's a young woman now, she must be twenty-three. But she's Kathleen sitting there. The years disappear and my palms begin to sweat. Inside, I feel myself curling into a ball, small enough so they can't hurt me.

Megan picks up the phone. On her hand, the skin is twisted and scarred. Guilt slams into me. I feel sick. She must see me shaking.

"June," she says into the cold, white mouthpiece.

I don't want to hear a voice that carries with it so many memories.

"Please," she clearly mouths.

I step forward, closer to her, and sit down on the chair. I don't take my eyes from her.

Her hair is darker than Kathleen's. Now that I'm this close, I can see thick make-up covering a scar melted onto her cheek and neck.

She starts to cry. She holds the phone tight to her ear and covers her eyes with her other hand.

I pick up the handset on this side. The sound of her tears fills the tiny room that I'm in. It's a sound that scorches my stomach. I keep my eyes wide open, because I know that if I close them I'll be dragged back to a darkness I don't know if I can escape.

"Megan, please," I say. She looks up, straight into my eyes. She's so slim still, her shoulders jutting out too sharply from her pink sweater.

"I'm sorry," she whispers. She holds tight to the telephone with both of her hands.

"I'm sorry, too," I say.

Megan takes a carefully folded tissue from her sleeve. I watch her, as though I've never seen her before. This strange, birdlike creature. I want to trace the outline of her on the glass. I think she's real, but she seems so different.

"I forgive you," I say. The words rush in and catch me by surprise.

"I forgive you too," she says, looking into my eyes.

I hesitate. "But your mother died because of me," I say.

"Yes," Megan answers. She stops crying and sits straighter in her chair and holds her shoulders back. "And you tried to kill me."

"No," I say instantly. "I never wanted to kill you." Never, never. That wasn't what I wanted to do.

"You lit a fire when we were asleep. You wanted us to die." Megan is crying again, but she doesn't look away from me. I can see every second of pain she has stored inside her.

"I didn't want you to die," I tell her.

"Then why didn't you wake me up? Why didn't you get us out in time?"

"I tried, but I was scared. I was just burning Kathleen's things. Your pictures." I think the shame and guilt might sweep me away. "It was a small fire and I thought it would go out. It was so quick."

Megan stares at me as I cry. The ugly scarring on her hand grips tight to the telephone.

"I wanted you all to get out," I say.

"My mom never woke up." She stares at me. "They say you lit the fire and sat on the lawn and watched."

"That's not true." I shake my head.

"That you hid the window keys out of reach. It took me so long to find the key, June," she cries. "I nearly didn't get out."

"It was Kathleen. She kept them above the curtain rails."

Megan nods and looks down at the table.

"She treated you badly," she says.

"But I didn't want her to die."

"I treated you badly." Megan pulls gently on the silver cord of the telephone.

"Yes," I say. "I was scared. All the time, I was scared."

Megan nods slowly.

"I was scared too," she says quietly.

I think any child living under Kathleen's roof would, at times, have been terrified, Reverend Shaw had told me.

"Is that why you did it?" I ask. "Why you hurt me too?"

"I'm sorry."

"Were you scared she'd do it to you?" I ask. I watch as Megan folds in on herself.

"Sometimes she did."

"Sometimes she did what?" I ask, but Megan doesn't reply. "Did Kathleen hurt you?" I go cold.

She nods.

"When?" I ask quietly, although I don't want to hear.

"When no one was looking," Megan says.

"I didn't know." I didn't see.

"No one knew."

"You didn't tell anyone?"

"I tried to tell you," she says. My heart stops. "But I didn't know how. And you were so scared of me that I couldn't come close."

My words feel tangled in mud and wire, and I can't find even one to speak.

"She built a wall between us," Megan says, so quietly. "And neither of us could get through."

I look at her on the other side of the glass. We're separated still, but I can see her clearly. And all I want to do is reach out for the little girl who was brought into my life. I want to change her ending and help her to fly.

"I didn't know that your dad was mine, too," she suddenly says. There's a strength in her eyes.

"Did you never suspect he was?"

"No. I promise." She doesn't look away from me as she shakes her head. "I believed Mom's story about my dad. He left me and didn't look back."

"But none of it was true."

"I always thought I wasn't good enough for him to stay," Megan says. "Mom said he didn't want me."

Years of lies and pain stack up bit by bit around us.

"And, all the time, our dad let me believe that," she says. "He knew how much it hurt me and he didn't say a thing."

"Maybe he thought you were too young to understand."

"No. I don't think he ever would have told me."

"He would." I want to believe it. "He just couldn't find the right words, at the right time."

"He was a coward." I feel her drifting away from me, into her own thoughts, and I want her to stay.

"Megan," I say, "if we have the same dad, it means that you're my real sister." I smile. She nods and I think she wants to speak, but she's crying too much. "And that wall that Kathleen built? I think we should knock it down."

AFTER
one month later

They came this morning to remove everything from my cell. I'm officially on Death Watch. I've got seven days left.

When I step back inside, I don't know where I am. My room is naked and it's not my own. They've taken everything. Every book I'd stacked neatly on the floor. Blister's photograph in its cardboard frame. And every letter that he wrote to me. Hundreds of his words, folded into envelopes. They've taken them all away.

I sit on the bed. I don't want to look at the door, but I do. It's empty of Blister's paper shapes. All fifty-seven of them are gone. The bars are bare. Every last bit of thread has been swept away.

They want it to be like I never existed.

An officer sits on the other side of the door. They will watch me, twenty-four hours a day. They will write down everything I do. I smile at him and he nods and smiles back.

His notes on me will be all that's left.

I turn on the faucet and bend down to wash my face. I feel into the plughole. My compass is wedged there. Gently, I pry it out.

I leave the water running. It sounds like a river. Over on the bed I lie down and press my damp face into the pillow.

Left or right, Blister?

. . .

I'm taken away from my cell into another small room. I stand with my arms high as they measure me and lower them when they need to do the length of my arms.

They don't tell me what it's for, but I know. They like the execution suit to fit properly, so that nothing can go wrong.

They sit me at a table and ask me what I want done with my body after I'm gone.

I will burn, just as my dad did.

They bring me back to my cell.

I can't eat the food they give me. I know that I should, because hunger only makes me feel worse, but today I can't. Today, I just stare at my blank door, where Blister's shapes should be.

And I look out the high-up window and hope to see a bird. Hope for it to swoop down and *peck peck peck* at the glass until there's a hole big enough for me to squeeze through. And I'll hold onto his wings and he'll take me away.

He'll take me to the gate by our trailers. I'll climb over, scraping my legs slightly on the rough wood. I'll walk down our path, with grass and aster flowers on either side. Blister will be there. He's older, but he looks up and he smiles and moves to make room for me on the step beside him. And together we sit, our faces looking to the sun.

   • • •

I have one more day and one more night in this cell before they move me to the Death House. It's a name I don't like and I won't use it again. I'm there for twenty-four hours. Until the end.

It's a forty-five-mile drive to get there. We will pass by trees and fields that I won't be able to see. I will hear other cars go by, but I won't know where they're going. I will never see the people inside them. They'll have no idea about me.

It's a beautiful day. The sunshine climbs through my window and settles on the bed. It's amazing how warm it can be, even through such a small piece of glass. It wants to get in, so it will.

I have to breathe slowly and count to ten, but it doesn't slow my heart down. It's beating so fast. It knows that it has such a short time left.

   • • •

It's strange being in a van. It's strange knowing that the outside world is just there. On the other side of this thin sheet of steel, there's freedom. But I can't get to it. Whatever I do, however hard I try, it's beyond my reach.

I recognize the sensation of the road running away from under us. The gentle rocking that makes me want to sleep.

Time is so strange. Some people think that it doesn't exist at all.

The years I've spent in my cell have been endless and yet so short. I don't know how I've filled my days. I don't know how the nights come around each time, but they always do.

Until tomorrow. Tomorrow, I won't go to bed and close my

eyes. I will not dream. I will not turn over in my sleep to face the other wall. The night won't come around again.

The van stops. They open the back door. I'm groggy as I step down. The sky is gray and the morning is still cold.

The ground is hard underneath my shoes. I can feel Blister's compass pressing into the sole of my foot.

They don't let me choose which way to go. They lead me straight ahead.

The air is thick with death. It's heavy on my skin. It's in the eyes of the officers. It's on their breath.

It's very quiet here. The corridor is empty, but for us. The sound of the keys grates inside me.

The door closes loudly.

The cell is too big. There's no window.

I wonder about the people who have been here before me. There's no sign of them anywhere.

I lie on the bed and stare at the blank ceiling until I see butterflies. Hundreds of paper butterflies flying silently together. The patterns in their wings have been carefully cut. I think they would break if I touched them.

• • •

I'm woken by the sound of the cell door opening. It's early morning.

The last day.

I can't stop myself from shaking.

The officer brings in my breakfast. He waits outside the door and watches me as I eat.

He watches me, as Kathleen used to, so that I finish every mouthful.

The officer takes away my empty plate. The chaplain walks in. I'm crushed that's it not my reverend, even though I knew that they wouldn't let him be with me at the end. Because he needs to live after today.

"I'm Reverend Miller." He is so young, too young to have to do this. I want to greet him, but the words don't come out. "Can I sit down?" he asks. I nod and he sits next to me on the bed. "Reverend Shaw told me you like him to read to you."

Reverend Shaw.

"Would you like me to?" the chaplain asks.

I nod.

He opens the thin pages of the Bible. And as he reads, I look at my hands. At my fingers grown older. I move my wrist, see the bones and rivers of veins underneath. Everything works. Nothing went wrong. My body didn't fail me and it wants to live.

Reverend Miller reaches out and holds my hand. He reads on, breathing calmly. I breathe with him. My blood goes into my heart and out again. It makes my lungs be filled with air.

I let my tears come. The feel of the pain in my chest and in my throat and the water on my cheeks. The salt touch on my lips.

I look at the reverend's kind face as he reads to me. I close my eyes and listen as the letters make up the words and they lift from the page and twist and duck above us.

"Though the mountains be shaken and the hills be removed, yet my unfailing love for you will not be shaken." His voice calms me. The words calm me.

"Do you believe I'll see her again?" I ask suddenly, opening my eyes. He puts his finger on the line in the page and looks up at me. "My mom died when I was young. Will I see her again?"

Reverend Miller thinks for a moment, before he replies. "Jesus answered him, 'Truly I tell you, today you will be with me in paradise.'"

"Does that mean yes?"

"I believe you'll see her again, June."

"Will she still love me?"

"Of course."

"Even after what I did?"

"Yes." He looks at me. "You are loved, June. You are precious."

"Then why do they want to kill me?" I ask him.

Reverend Miller sighs. "I suppose they think that by taking your life it will even things out."

"Does that make them murderers too?"

"I think it's very complicated."

"Will they really do it?"

He doesn't reply. The air buzzes between us.

Time passes. The reverend stays with me.

An officer brings in a meal I no longer want.

Reverend Miller reads to me.

The words are all.

The officer takes away the cold, jellied food I have not touched.

I see Reverend Miller glance at his watch.

"What time is it?" I ask. He sits up straight, but I can see what's in his eyes.

"You haven't long, June," he says.

I look at him for such a long time. I almost reach out to touch the skin on his face.

"Will you tell Reverend Shaw something for me?" I ask.

"Of course."

"Will you tell him that I forgive Kathleen?" I'm surprised how strong my voice is. And how as soon as I say the words a dark knot in my chest begins to loosen. "If I'm not a monster, maybe she wasn't either."

"I think you're right," Reverend Miller says.

"Maybe she didn't mean to." I want so much to make sense, to be understood. "She wasn't born bad, either," I tell him.

"No," he says, "I don't think she was. I don't think anyone is."

"And will you tell Reverend Shaw that I forgive my father for not seeing?"

"I will," he says.

In an instant, I remember my dad sitting at the top of the High Point. The wind pushes his hair from his face as he smiles at me. He is alive and he loves me. It's how it was. It's how it should always have been.

"And what about you, June? Can I tell him that you've forgiven yourself?"

I shake my head. "I still don't know how." I want to see his face clearly, but my tears are washing him away.

"Forgiveness is easy," he says. "It's just like a door. You open it and walk through."

"Am I allowed, though?"

"You are," he says. "In fact, it's the right thing to do."

I close my eyes and listen to the beating of my heart and the whisper of my breath.

And I push open the heavy door and step through.

"You won't be forgotten, June," Reverend Miller says. "Many people will remember you. There were protestors outside here all night."

"For me?" I open my eyes and look at him again.

"Yes. I have photographs, if you'd like to see."

To see a picture of strangers who don't want me to die? People I don't know and will never meet. People who stood in the cold as I slept.

"Yes," I say.

Reverend Miller takes a photograph from the pocket inside his jacket and he passes it to me.

It shows a crowd of people, holding candles against the night.

"They really came here for me?" I whisper.

"Yes."

I breathe in sharply. Because there, in the middle, is Blister. He looks older. His hair is short again and he's wearing his glasses. I touch the photograph. He's just there. My Blister.

In his hand, he holds a candle. I stare at him and see all the years that he never gave up on me.

Mr. and Mrs. Wick are standing beside him. They've aged a hundred years. I touch their faces. The sadness in them floods my skin. I have so much that I want to say to them. I have so much that I want them to say to me. But they honored my wish. They stopped visiting when I asked. I never answered their letters. I never told them how much they meant to me and how the words they wrote to me became boats that kept me afloat. And I only didn't reply because the pain blinded me.

Maggie is there too. Older, more sensible-looking, but still Maggie. I search the faces. Mil, Si, Chubbers, Eddie— they're all there. I look for Tom, although I know I won't find him. I try to imagine the young man he would have become, tall and slim, with a look in his eyes like Blister used to have. I have spent so many days, years, holding his hand tight as he drifted away.

I should have been with him.

And there, at the side, is my sister.

"You came," I whisper to Megan, but, as the wasted years crush me, I can't say anymore.

"June?" Reverend Miller's voice is here, but I hold onto the photograph.

I make myself look again at Blister. I touch his lips. I wish I could make him smile. My eyes meet his.

Keep fighting for others like me, I tell him.

Blister looks at me. The candle he holds is bright against the dark.

I've got my compass, I tell him. *It'll show me the way.*

There's a sudden ringing in the corridor. A strange, distorted phone, which shatters my calm. Reverend Miller looks up quickly and walks to the bars of the cell. An officer is speaking. His back is toward us. Another woman officer rushes to stand beside him. She looks at me, but I don't understand the expression on her face.

The officer replaces the telephone's handset in the hook on the wall. He turns around and walks toward me. Is he coming to get me? Is it my time?

I get up and go to stand next to Reverend Miller. My hands are with his, on the cold bars that cut up the corridor outside.

The officer's lips are moving. I know he's saying words, but they seem like only fragments. None of them makes sense.

I look to the reverend. I'm shaking as he turns to me and takes both my shoulders in his hands. His eyes are telling me something I can't grasp.

He doesn't say anything for a moment. My heart is thumping, but the rhythm feels all wrong. "You've been granted a stay of execution, June," he says. His words are framed by a smile.

"What do you mean?" Nothing makes sense. There's a ringing in my ears that won't go away.

"You're not going to die today."

I'm trying to speak again, to form words, but they won't appear.

"A new lawyer has stepped in, to represent you," the officer says. He's smiling too. I think he's genuinely happy. "She's arguing that you've had inadequate representation."

"I don't understand," I finally say. I look down at the sleeves of my execution suit. "They've made this for me."

"And someone has come forward with new evidence."

"Who?"

"I haven't any more details," the officer says.

Reverend Miller's smile shines. "Your new lawyer will fight for you to live, June."

I look up at him. His face becomes clearer. I think I know what he's trying to say. I look down at my hands. I have a small scratch underneath the knuckle of my thumb, pink against my dark skin. Now, it'll have time to heal.

I put my hand on my chest and feel my heart beating, steadily now. I'll go to sleep tonight with it still beating. And I'll wake up tomorrow.

I can feel Blister's compass under the sole of my foot.

"Which way, June?" I hear him ask. *"You choose."*

The compass presses its circle into my skin as Reverend Miller puts his arms around me.

I choose life, Blister.

I choose life.

A NOTE FROM BLISTER

June once thought that a butterfly would die if you touched its wings. I didn't know then whether it was true, but I know now that it's not. I've learned that if you're careful, you can hold a butterfly in your hand. And that even if it's been trapped, frightened, in a jar, it has a chance to survive. Because a butterfly with a broken wing can still fly.

I've also learned that a proper legal team changes everything.

That a sister's love can keep your heart beating.

That truth can win.

That sometimes best friends are more than that. And if you hold hands tight, you can run blind through any storm.

And I've learned that with a blank piece of paper, you can do anything.

Acknowledgments

The biggest thank you of all is to my wonderful mum. You gave me the wings to fly. I love you and I miss you.

Thank you, Miles, for living with a crazy lady who sees people that you don't. And to our truly gorgeous boys, Frank, Arthur and Albert—you make my day, everyday.

To Philip, Lara, Emma and Anna—thank you for your endless enthusiasm for my dream. I'm so proud to call you my siblings.

Thank you to my AMAZING agent, Veronique Baxter. Your support and encouragement consistently astounds me—I feel more than lucky to have you by my side. And thank you to the rest of the brilliant team at David Higham—the lovely Laura West, Nikoline Eriksen and my foreign rights experts Alice Howe, Emily Randle and Emma Jamison.

To my dream-team of editors, Ali Dougal and Lindsey Heaven—thank you for loving June and Blister so completely and for making my book what it is today. It's been amazing to work with you both and I thank my lucky stars that you're at the helm.

To my disco hero, Ben Hughes. Your covers for my books are the most beautiful I've ever seen. I can never thank you enough. And a huge thank you to everyone at Egmont, especially Maggie Eckel for your kindness, patience and encouragement and Emily Thomas for spreading the word far and wide. And Lucy Pearce, for loving June's story early on.

To Lucy Howe—thank you for being the most amazing friend a girl could have. And Martyn, the king of firework lighting!

Thank you, wonderful Whinneys, for encircling my family with so much love. And to Toots—for Bobby McGee and swinging to the stars. To Er (@mercytree_mum), for having a heart as big as the world and proving that there are enough hours in the day. Mari, for the strong roots of your friendship. To Jill, Cami, Evé and Louie, for the love, laughs and big pants.

Thank you, Allie, Debs, Lucy, Sandi and Suzanna, for showing me how it's done. And a big thank you to Nikki for your edgeless love and support. And to Tash, for evenings spent dissecting the strange writing world we're in.

Thank you to the following, just for being brilliant— Stephen Nash, Shanaz, Nicky M-M, Andrew, Jo Sykes, Sam, Rosie, Francoise, Fabia, Cathy and Carlene, Laura Treneer, Lou, Ula and Becky.

To Abi, for showing us that when life serves you a stinking curve-ball, you can hold your head high and walk a happier path.

To Jo—for fighting with such courage. You'll always be loved and missed. And Tony, for showing incredible strength— I'm lucky to call you my friend.

Thank you to all the amazing bloggers, for your time, energy and passion. In particular to the super-lovely Michelle Toy (Tales Of Yesterday), whose opinion I value greatly. And Jim (YA Yeah! Yeah!), Lucy (Queen Of Contemporary), Viv (Serendipity Reviews), The YA Fictionados, Lisa (City Of YA Books) and Carly (Writing From The Tub).

To Ness and Jules at The Book Nook—thank you for championing my books from the word go!

To the original "Seedlings"—LD Lapinski, Oliver Clark and Sana Aslam. Your support has bowled me over. I hope to be able to do the same for you one day!

And finally, thank you to June for finding my writing spirit. Your story humbled me and broke me in equal measures. I hope I've done it justice.